Forever Hot

SOMETIMES YOU HAVE TO START OVER.

When her late husband's family almost abducts her two-year-old daughter, trauma counselor Glenna Carnes knows she has only one real choice. It is time to leave Finley Creek behind—and start a new life elsewhere.

Glenna makes the difficult decision to ask for help getting out of Finley Creek for good. Her friends have *one* place in mind where they know Glenna and her three little girls can build the life Glenna has always dreamed about for her children:

Masterson County.

She just had to find a job there first. And a place to live. *Fast.*

Phil Tyler seems like the best solution…

Forever Holding Phil

FOR EVERYTHING THERE IS A SEASON...

CALLE J. BROOKES

LOST RIVER LIT PUBLISHING, LLC

FOREVER HOLDING *PHIL*

Copyright © 2022 by Calle J. Brookes

PBFV

ISBN: 978-1-940937-50-2

For information contact: www.callejbrookes.com

Book and Cover design by C.J. BROOKES

First Edition: MAY2022

06142022

10 9 8 7 6 5 4 3 2 1

One

THERE CAME A TIME WHEN YOU HAD TO MAKE A choice.

This was one of them.

"I'm going to have to do something."

Glenna Carnes stared at the four women surrounding her as the words seared themselves into her soul. She couldn't keep doing this to her daughters.

All Glenna wanted was for her daughters to feel safe. *This* was just proof that she was failing miserably at that task.

Emmaline was still crying. Emmy—her tough one. Her middle child who had never been afraid of anything before. Today she had been terrified by a delivery man.

Glenna scooped her up and rocked her, meeting the eyes of her two closest friends, and the two other women at W4HAV, the women's charity where she worked as a trauma counselor. They all knew this couldn't keep going on. This *fear* was destroying her baby girls. "I...this is getting out of hand. I can't seem to avoid them anywhere. I have to do something."

The delivery man hadn't been one of her former brothers-in-law, but Emmy hadn't known that. All her almost five-year-old daughter remembered about the uncle who had shown up in the front yard four months ago screaming that Glenna owed them something was that he had been dressed in a private-delivery-company uniform. That had been enough to have her little girl screaming today. Between that and the way her seven-year-old Evangeline flinched each time the telephone rang and her two-and-a-half-year-old baby Eleanor cried and resisted whenever Glenna tried to leave her in the co-op nursery room now...

The girls weren't getting over their fears—they were just getting worse.

She had to do something.

Glenna looked at Robin and Rory, her two closest friends on the planet. Her sisters of the heart. Rory had scooped Elly into her own arms and was rocking her, too.

Her most empathetic baby always cried when one of her sisters was upset.

Evey watched from the doorway to the children's playroom at W4HAV, a leery look on her beautiful face. One filled with suspicion. Fear. Worry that no child her age should have.

It was the last straw.

Her ex's family wasn't anywhere near them now—not that she knew, anyway, but she wouldn't put it past them—but their constant harassment of *her* was destroying her daughters' sense of safety and peace.

She wouldn't have it. Not any longer.

She'd do anything for her daughters.

She looked at the women surrounding her. She knew how the charity operated—knew what it was capable of. And Lacy, the blond woman next to her, had been trying to talk her into asking for *help* for weeks. "I need to find a place to get away for a while. Build a new life for the four of us. Where they don't have to be afraid of their father's family any longer."

It wasn't running, exactly. It was *relocating*. Doing what was best for her daughters.

Even though it meant leaving everything, everyone, she knew behind.

"I have to do this. Before I change my mind."

"Where are you going to go?" Robin asked, tears filling her big blue eyes. Tears—and understanding. Robin and Rory knew her struggles, knew exactly what battle she had been fighting for just too long…

Robin's own two-year-old daughter was in the playroom with Robin's nine-year-old twin boys. Innocent children, too.

Children who had experienced far too much pain already.

All Glenna wanted was for them to grow up in a world without this kind of fear and hurt and loss. If she could keep that from touching her girls, she would do whatever it took.

"I…I don't know. I just know I have to get them away from here for a while. So that they can learn not to be afraid." Her heart broke for her daughters. She'd tried everything from confronting her ex's family to speaking with an attorney about restraining orders against all of them.

She'd filed a report with Detective Acardi, a friend of Rory's, after the latest incident.

He had told her the Texas State Police could make a case for attempted kidnapping, but her ex-mother-in-law would probably plead it down to maintaining a common nuisance or something trivial like that.

Never mind that Elly had had dreams of the scary lady trying to take her away every night since. Nothing Glenna did could fix that.

"I have a brother, but…he lives on a military base. I don't want to impose on him." Her half brother would let them stay with him for a while, but it would be awkward for them all. They weren't exactly close.

"Let W4HAV find you a place," Lacy said for about the fifteenth time in a week. "It's what we do."

"I know." She didn't *want* to need that kind of help. There were women out there who needed the escape the women's charity provided far more than Glenna did. Abused women who needed to get away however they could. Abused men, too, who came to W4HAV for help, though far fewer men would admit they needed the help than women.

Glenna was a respected mental health counselor; she led four different counseling groups for the charity at two o'clock, four days each week. She worked the intake desk four nights a week from three thirty p.m. until nine, when she took the girls home and put them to bed. She had a small home she had purchased on Boethe Street after she'd paid off half of her student debt, and then she'd paid that house and her remaining debt off with the life insurance policy she'd still had on her ex at the time of his death over two years ago.

She had a good job, her bills were paid, there was a roof over their heads, and her children were safe. They should have been just fine.

But *they weren't*.

Her ex's family could get to them at any time.

His mother walking into the church multipurpose room where the homeschool co-op met each week and nearly walking out with Elly had just proven that.

There had been a homeschool dad Glenna had known well in the parking lot who had seen what was happening—and stopped it. Just in time. She had been lucky he had recognized Elly that day and stepped in to make a difference. Had questioned.

Glenna hadn't slept well since.

Her arms tightened around Emmy. Her bright, fiery, passionate, brave little girl who would challenge the world just because she could.

Crying because of a package left on the desk at W4HAV.

Glenna understood how trauma worked, though she didn't work with children in her groups. She wasn't going to see the trauma of their father's death get compounded with her own children because of his family.

That was one thing he had been adamant about when she'd filed for divorce—he hadn't wanted his mother or three brothers anywhere near the girls. No matter what. That had been something he and Glenna had actually agreed on.

Lincoln's mother didn't believe that. And she was determined to get to the girls, no matter what.

"I need someplace to go. Even if it means I'm washing dishes for a living for a while. I need to get out of Finley Creek. Before they destroy my daughters even more."

Lacy asked for her to give her a day or two to work things out. To find some options that would suit Glenna and the girls.

Glenna knew how it worked. There was a fund that no one talked about.

The escape fund.

It was designed to help those victims of violence who had no real recourse but to run.

Glenna wasn't like that.

The same procedures in place for that, would help her now.

She looked at her children one more time. Yes. She would do whatever she had to for her girls. Anything.

Even if it meant leaving everything behind.

Two

HE WASN'T DEAD YET. AT FIFTY, PHILIP TYLER KNEW HE still had a lot of kick left in him. Even if it didn't feel like it, all the time. He was too damned tired for this constant traveling between Masterson, Wyoming and Finley Creek, Texas. That was becoming clearer every time.

It was time he figured something else out.

He had a plan—go home, let his nephew Fletcher buy in to his partnership with Travis Worthington-Deane in Texas, and hire himself a housekeeper.

So he could spend more time with the four daughters and three sons he had in Masterson. His seven grandkids and any others that came along. And his oldest son, whenever that boy bothered to come back in from L.A. where he was making his own way in the world.

Phil wanted time with his family.

Phil wasn't going to *retire* exactly. He was going to slow things down some. He'd accomplished what he'd set out to do with this partnership. His ranch was secure, for whichever of his kids took it over eventually. He had paid down most of his debts, and had put a little back in case some of the younger kids needed help with college.

He had finished what he'd set out to do. That didn't mean he was dead yet, though.

Now it was time to sit back and enjoy it. Enjoy the remainder of his younger kids' childhoods while he still had that opportunity. And get to know the boy who was almost a man before it was too late.

Phil had taken Lacy and Travis up on their offer to spend another night with them after he'd not been able to get a flight in time the night before. He enjoyed himself. They were good kids. Good friends. He considered them family, too.

He was fond of them both, even if little Lacy, a blond dynamo a few years older than Phil's eldest girl, was nervous with any man not her husband or his brothers when they got too close into her space. She was getting better with him, poor kid. After nearly dying in much the same way as Phil's third daughter, Perci.

Lacy reminded him of Perci.

Both girls had that same fighting spirit.

It had given him time to talk with them about his plans for the next few months.

Or rather, his lack of plans. Phil was looking forward to it. Thanks to money he and Travis had earned through their risks, he had some extra cash. Cash he intended to use to fix up the house and barns a bit. He wanted to tackle the basement, finally. He and his late wife, Becky, had planned for years to finish it out and make a genuine family space down there for the kids.

He suspected Pete would stick around once he turned eighteen in six months, though. Phil was hoping. His second son was a rancher born and bred. He didn't see Pete going anywhere too far away. If that was what his son wanted, then so be it. Phil would support him.

Just as he'd supported Phoenix's move to Hollywood of all places. His oldest son had left after they'd used Phil's ranch as a location shoot two and a half years ago. Phoenix was making his own way there.

Phil thought leaving Masterson was probably the best for Phoenix, but not having one of his children right there stung.

Phil thought about that as he and Travis headed toward the women's charity Lacy volunteered at several nights a week.

He was hoping to meet his new housekeeper there. Lacy had talked with him quietly the evening before. Had asked him to consider a woman she'd known for years.

He was there to do a favor for Lacy. That was it.

Travis's daughter babbled at him as they walked up the sidewalk toward the charity. Phil laughed.

The sight of little Alonna with her white-blond hair sticking up everywhere, and her little plaid shirt and denim overalls was cute. Made him miss his grandchildren. All seven of them, from five-year-old Ivy all the way down to the newest, Griffen.

Phil would admit it—he was a homebody family man. He wanted to go home, and *know* he didn't have to go anywhere for a while if he didn't want to.

He'd turned his rental car in already—Travis was going to drop him off at the airport after he dropped the baby off with Lacy.

At W4HAV. Phil had heard great things about it but had never been there himself.

His niece Maggie had stayed with Travis's in-laws for a few months after some trouble in Masterson. She'd received counseling there at the charity that she said had helped her through a great deal.

He was going to make a small donation while he was there. It was the least he could do for the place that had helped his Maggie.

And if he could help Lacy help someone else in need, then Phil was going to damned well do it.

He saw the woman they were looking for the instant he opened the door to the charity and stepped inside.

Lacy stood near the receptionist desk speaking with a woman who looked so much like Phil's daughters Pip and Perci that he did a double take.

And then he couldn't believe what he was seeing at all. *Who* he was seeing.

Three

"*Phil!*"

Phil opened his arms, and the woman jumped straight into them. He wrapped her up tight and just held her.

As everyone around them stared. He just held her. Remembered her as a scrawny, terrified kid so long ago. Finally, she pulled back. Wiped her wet cheeks.

Phil ignored the crowd around him.

He got his first real look at his late wife's baby sister. She had put on a bit of weight, but not much. Still was on the small side.

Her sister had been the same way. His daughters all took after that side of their family.

Robin's hair was the same burnished red as three of Phil's daughters, and three of his sons'. Her eyes were a lighter shade of blue. He and Becky had both been blue-eyed redheads. Their children had been bound to inherit the same.

Seeing Robin was like seeing Becky all over again. Twenty years—it had been twenty years, now. He'd heard rumors she'd returned to Masterson fifteen years ago, but it hadn't been her.

He'd looked for her. They'd missed her so damned much. Especially her sister.

But she was in front of him right now.

"I didn't realize you were in Finley Creek."

"I bounced around a bit...after I left...and ended up here. Built a life here. Married. I'm a widow, now. Three years ago."

He suspected it was more complicated than she was making it out to be. Phil looked at the people surrounding them. Even little Alonna was watching them. He saw the obvious confusion. "Robin is my late wife's younger sister. She had to leave Masterson twenty years or so ago after some trouble with the former sheriff. We haven't seen her since. Or really even known where she was. One hell of a coincidence finding her here."

Once again, an oversimplification of what had been an extremely tense situation, and Robin had been no more than eighteen at the time.

Phil had put her on the bus out of town himself, with four hundred borrowed dollars and a prayer. He would never forget how that moment had felt.

"You needing a job, Robbie? It's yours. Come on home." He had had to help her leave, because he had had no other way to protect her back then.

"I'm not the one for the job, Phil. But...my best friend, Glenna...is." She stepped aside, and he got his first good look at the woman sitting at the table behind her.

She was around the same age as Robin, maybe a bit older. But was around three inches taller and a bit curvier. But not much. She was a pretty woman, one who would probably age very well. And there was a fear, a sadness, in her eyes that Phil didn't like to see.

It was far too similar to what had been in his second daughter's eyes not that long ago.

The woman stood. Stared at him out of beautiful green eyes. She held out a hand. "Hello, I'm Glenna Carnes, Robin's best friend. I'm the one who...Lacy...told me you are looking for a housekeeper to help with your children."

Phil wrapped his fingers around hers. She had a very soft, feminine hand. Delicate and silk beneath his work-roughened fingers. "Yes. I will be honest. It's not a high-paying job. I simply can't afford it now. And the work will only be part-time now. I am throwing in room and board as part of the deal."

"I'd...need that. I want to start completely fresh somewhere away from Finley Creek. I am not a housekeeper by trade, though I worked my way through college with my own cleaning business eighteen years ago. I know what the work involves."

"Glenna is a licensed mental health counselor here," Lacy, his business partner's wife, said quietly. "She's intending to transfer her license to wherever she settles eventually. That will take time. She'll need a job in the meantime. I thought the two of you could help each other."

Phil nodded. He hadn't had any intention of interviewing a housekeeper tonight. He'd wanted to wait a few weeks after he got home. Talk to the boys—he still had three at home, ranging from almost eighteen down to his youngest at ten—see what kind of a woman they wanted living in their house.

When Lacy had come to him, telling him of a woman who needed a bit of help for a while, Phil had had to say yes. He was the kind of man who did what he could to help those who needed it.

Finding Robin again was just a miracle that he had never expected to have again.

"What kind of job do you have in Masterson?" Robin asked quietly.

Glenna stepped forward, shooting him a shy look that had him feeling a bit protective. She did have that air about her just like his daughter Pip had once had. "I should tell you before this goes any further. If you offered me the job, I wouldn't come alone. I have three children. Girls. Ages seven, almost five, and two-and-a-half."

That was something he hadn't counted on. He also saw the fear in her eyes.

The desperation.

She wanted out of Finley Creek. And Robin and Lacy were trying to help her.

"I need someone to help me with the ranch now. The house, I mean. And the boys. It's not fair to keep putting it on the girls when they are trying to build their own lives, their own families. I need someone I can trust, but I can't afford much more than room and board. I can feed extra mouths, Mrs. Carnes. Food's not the problem. And I have extra bedrooms. I was planning on hiring someone when I got home. Pip and Phoebe usually help with the boys, but they have four kids between them now. I can't keep asking this of my girls. I'm a fair employer, and the ranch is a safe place for kids. I've made sure of that years ago. There will be room for them to play and grow. They'll be treated as honorary Tylers. And it'll get you far away from Texas, if that's what you're wanting. For as long as you are needing it to."

MC

GLENNA DIDN'T SEE where she had much choice. Not if she wanted to take the girls someplace *safe*. Lacy had called her late the night before and told her she had a job in mind for her. That Lacy was one hundred percent certain the job would be perfect for her—and would provide exactly the safety she was looking for her girls.

Glenna wanted that so much. They couldn't even play in the yard without fear that Lincoln's crazy family would drive by and harass them again. They lived three blocks away. His family walked by her house every single day.

After they tried to take Elly, Glenna hadn't been able to sleep at night, afraid they'd break in and take one—or all—of the girls. She and the girls could just leave—just pack up the rest of their things, load a rental truck and just...go.

To Masterson.

Leaving Rory and Robin. To even think of that was like the idea of tearing off a limb.

They were her family, too.

"It is beautiful there," Robin said. She had spoken of home so many times, but the reason why she had left had always been a secret. "Go there, Glenna. It's a wonderful place."

"Room for you and yours, too, Robin. There always will be. And don't you ever forget it. We can do some shifting around, and if the kids wouldn't mind doubling up, there are plenty of bedrooms. The house may be small, but it was built for a family."

Glenna looked over at her children, at her three little girls playing together, with Robin's daughter's bright strawberry-red head in the middle of them. The boys, older, strong and sturdy, played a board game. They were laughing, having fun. Being children.

She lived in a tiny house on Boethe Street. Robin was just three doors down. They were still trying to fight with insurance companies more than a year after the tornado, just to make the rest of the repairs. Half of Robin's windows were still covered with plywood. Their yards were tiny, not much room for children to run and play. Boethe Street wasn't the kind of place you let your children play unattended either.

Not like the place this man had described.

His name was Philip Tyler. He'd been married to Robin's sister Rebecca. Robin's children: Philip, Wesley Tyler, and Rebecca.

Her best friend had missed her family so much she'd named her children after them.

She looked at him, wondering what she should say next. Lacy Deane's baby reached for him, and he took her. Naturally. Like he'd held her a hundred times before.

She just wanted someplace where she and her girls could *relax*. Not worry about someone gossiping about something they'd done to Lincoln's mother or brothers.

The petty harassment his family repeatedly dished out to her and her daughters was sickening. They walked by her house all the time. Calling to her, calling to the girls. Nothing she'd done had been able to stop them.

Rory had even asked a few friends from the TSP to talk to them. It hadn't helped.

If a six-foot-four, angry detective from Major Crimes couldn't stop them from harassing her, nothing could.

She just wanted to get away from it. Here was a man that her best friend was telling her she could trust offering her exactly that.

She just had to make a deal with a total stranger to make it happen.

Four

SHE WAS REALLY GOING TO DO THIS.

"Are you certain I can trust him with the girls?" Glenna asked. Robin and Rory were with her, helping her pack a few essentials. It was almost time.

To make one of the biggest changes of her life.

In a single day, thanks to W4HAV, she had made all the arrangements she needed. Anything else could be done on the internet and phone. Rory was going to help with that.

"I'd give Phil my children in a heartbeat if I needed to put them somewhere safe, Glenna. In an instant. He'd do whatever he had to for the kids. That's the kind of man he is. I can't think of a better place for you to start over." Robin gave a soft, quiet smile. A sad one. One filled with so many memories and dreams gone.

"You've never said why you left Wyoming," Rory said. "But I know it was bad."

"It was. Becky and I, we didn't have that great of a home life. She met Phil when she was nineteen and I was almost ten. She fell hard. Told me she just knew that he was the man she was meant to marry. He was just as hung up on her. They got pregnant—my father went through the roof. He kicked Becky out. She and Phil married two weeks later. They moved into his grandfather's old house. It was so tiny, half the size of my house now. Two bedrooms no bigger than closets. Eventually, they moved into his father's old house; by that point, they'd had five kids. I was eighteen. I think Phil was around thirty and Becky twenty-seven. They were still very much in love. Phil adored her. I hope that never changed."

She paused for a long moment. When she looked back at Glenna her cheeks were wet. "There was this man...the sheriff. He liked younger women. Redheads, especially. He started harassing me, showing up everywhere I went. I was only four years older than his oldest son, and I wanted nothing to do with him. He was everywhere I turned. For weeks. He harassed Phil and Becky. Harassed Phil's younger brother Nick. The sheriff thought I was involved with Nick. One night after I was done working my shift at the inn, this sheriff pulled me over. He made me get out of my car while he interrogated me about who I had been with. We were all alone on the highway. That was one of the most terrifying nights of my life.

"Phil drove by and realized what was happening. He and Nick were together. They got out of their truck and just stood there. Watching. The sheriff yelled at Phil to get back in his truck and quit interfering with police business. Thank God we were on the edge of their brother Bill's property. He had no right to make them leave. They leaned up against Bill's fence and just watched. We'd tried to file harassment charges and do whatever we could, but he just wouldn't leave me alone.

"We knew after that night it wasn't going to end. Who do you go to when the man stalking you is the man you're supposed to report that kind of thing to? Phil was afraid what would happen if it escalated. So, Phil put me on the bus with four hundred dollars in my pocket. And I left."

Glenna felt sick just imagining it. "What about your parents?"

"What parents? By this time, they had already washed their hands of me—I was apparently too much trouble for them. They were done being parents. I had moved in with Becky three years earlier, at fifteen. Phil made me do my homework and set me a curfew, made me get a job so I could have my own money and feel independent. All the things I did not have at home. But...Phil was my hero. I want my boys to grow up to be the kind of man he is. To know him. I can't think of a better role model for young boys."

"Well, he's definitely hot enough. He can be Glenna's hero, too," Rory said, rolling her eyes in appreciation. "Thump, thump, thump. Did you see those shoulders? And those dark blue eyes. Wow."

Glenna's cheeks flamed as Robin burst into laughter. "I am not going to Masterson County, Wyoming, to drool over my new boss, Rory."

"Why not? I drool over my bosses all the time. Chief Marshall is extremely drool-worthy. As is the head of major crimes, and the major crimes supervisors, and some of the men in major crimes, and...I mean, I don't plan to ever date a red-haired man ever again—thank you, ex-husband Keaton-the-Cheatin'—but I can so appreciate when one is ruggedly handsome with broad shoulders, a tiny hiney, and has a warm, mellow voice that gives a woman shivers."

"Rory! That's my brother-in-law. That's so wrong. Wow."

"Tell me: Are all the Tylers like that? That one was definitely worth appreciating." Rory made an exaggerated eye roll. Being silly.

Distracting Glenna from what tomorrow would bring. She was the most anxious one of their little trio and always had been. Even though she was a few years older than the other women—they had always tried to protect her.

Glenna was going to miss them so much.

"Well, the ones I remember were. Most were married by that point. Only Nick wasn't. And while he could make any woman drool, he was a bit of jerk back then. Arrogant. Never could stand him and his cocky ways—even if he could kiss better than anyone I'd ever kissed before. Or since, for that matter. Come to think of it…"

"You kissed his brother?" Rory asked. "Do tell."

"I was young. Stupid. Learned my lesson there." She went on to tell the story with what Glenna suspected was a lot of exaggeration.

They spent the rest of the evening talking and laughing and taking care of their kids. Glenna felt like she was grieving in a way. Like she was losing a part of her world now.

One that she had clung to for a really long time.

Tonight, it felt like goodbye.

Robin and Rory were her support system. Her family. All she had, other than her babies. Even more than her brother, who she rarely saw. To know she was making this kind of change and they wouldn't be right by her side the whole way—it terrified her.

Glenna wasn't the *leader* of their group. Not at all. That was Rory, and to some extent Robin. No. Not Glenna. She was the quiet peacemaker of their little trio.

Rory promised to head to Masterson the first chance she could. She was going to bank up her comp time from the TSP. So she could stay for a week or two.

And Robin was going to dip into her savings and bring her children home. So they could meet their family, this summer. They had a plan. This was just temporary.

She would see them again. In just a few months. That was all.

If she and the girls liked it there, she'd transfer her licensing to Wyoming. Get a job in her chosen field. For now, she had a job waiting on her, a roof over her girls' heads, with a man she thought she could reasonably trust not to be a serial killer or anything.

She had more than a lot of women leaving W4HAV had.

She would have to remember that.

That didn't make it any easier to sleep after she'd sat the girls down and told them they were going on an adventure, though. They'd been full of questions and afraid. They'd only gotten *less* afraid when she'd told them they were going to stay with Becky, Philip, and Wesley's uncle and cousins when they got to where they were going.

Then she'd had to explain what cousins were. Because they didn't have any of their own.

Emmy was convinced a cousin was someone like the cousin in Harry Potter. That hadn't made the conversation easier. It had taken a while to convince her otherwise.

This felt like one of the scariest moments of her life—next to the day she'd decided that divorcing Lincoln was the best move she could make for the girls and herself.

That had been the right thing to do. She just hoped this was as well.

Five

HER FIRST SIGHT OF MASTERSON COUNTY, WYOMING, had her breath catching. It was...perfect. Just as quaint and welcoming as Robin had promised.

It had been a long few days on the road; she and the girls were utterly exhausted. No doubt, her new employer was as well. He'd offered to drive the small moving truck with her belongings in it, instead of W4HAV hiring a company to do it for her.

Phil had insisted he could do it. He hadn't said much when they'd stopped for meals together, or to give the girls time to play. She got the sense he wasn't much of a talker overall. He'd surprised her by playing kickball with the girls at one rest stop the day before, even though he'd obviously been tired.

He'd also carried a sleeping Emmy for her once, too, while she'd carried Elly.

She couldn't remember a time her girls had ever played so casually with a man. It made her feel a little odd. She'd watched them closely. She didn't know this man. She had agreed to move her daughters into his home.

That never made a woman feel super-safe right away.

He'd offered to pay for her hotel room, saying it was part of the relocation benefit, but she'd had funds from W4HAV for that very thing. Glenna would pay the charity back someday. Even if she just put one hundred dollars a month back until she had enough to send to the charity, she would.

She'd used most of her savings to bury Lincoln two years ago and then to buy the house and pay off debts he'd run up during their marriage. The small life insurance policy had only gone so far. She would pay the loan from W4HAV back, even though the charity never asked it.

So someone else who needed the help could have it.

He pulled over in front of a small diner, then came to her window. "Our place is down a winding road that can be a bit narrow. It's a service road called Tyler Road. It'll show up on GPS if we get separated. Make sure to give me plenty of room. Sudden stops happen out there. The curves can come up on you pretty suddenly, so watch yourself. I'm about forty miles south of here. This is the county seat. There is a strip mall a mile or so out, where the fast-food places are, but this here is the heart of Masterson. I'm going to walk up the street, put in a few orders for pizza to be delivered in a few hours. You all like pizza and breadsticks?"

Her girls did—it was their favorite, and frozen pizzas just weren't the same. "I can pitch in."

"Nonsense, I'm the one surprising my girls with four beautiful extra mouths to feed—and I'm going to talk to them about finding their aunt. It's going to be a bit of a celebration tonight. We've worried over Robin for a long, long time."

He hadn't exaggerated about the road. It was curvy and narrow and dark.

She just told the girls to be as quiet as they could, and she followed his taillights, white-knuckling the wheel the entire time.

Finally, they pulled into a long driveway that had been

freshly graveled, she suspected.

He parked the moving truck and blew the horn.

Glenna took her first look around.

The house had been freshly painted, and there were flowers popping through melting snow. There didn't seem to be much rhyme or reason for some of the additions that had obviously been made to the house throughout the years.

It was charming. Welcoming in a way that she couldn't quite understand.

The sun would be setting soon, but there was plenty of light to take in the place.

There was an old dog limping toward the steps, barking at them excitedly. A younger dog stood at her side almost protectively.

To Glenna's shock, a baby goat was casually chewing on something right in the middle of the sidewalk.

"Mommy, Mommy," Elly said, almost bouncing in her car seat. "Horsies. Sheepies!"

"That's a goat, Elly," Evey said, disgust in her tone. Evey, who knew everything and was sometimes impatient with her younger sisters. "There's a difference. Are we here at Mr. Phil's? Where are his little girls?"

"Honey, his daughters are grown-ups, I think. They are all mommies themselves. He has sons that are a little older than you, though."

"Oh. I thought there would be little girls to play with."

"I'm afraid not."

Evangeline was most certainly put out by *that*. "Who are we going to play with then?"

Well, child number one wasn't happy. "I don't know. Maybe there will be other kids? I don't know people around here, remember? We're all going to have to make new friends."

"Can we ride the goat?" Emmy, her most adventurous child, asked. Glenna knew what she was thinking with just one look.

The poor goats. They were probably in for the shock of their lives, once her girls got settled in.

"Absolutely not. No riding anything with legs."

"I bet the dogs will bite us. And eat Elly."

Evey, again. Of course. It was always Evey.

"No one is going to get eaten." Glenna pulled in a deep breath. It was time to get them out of the SUV—before they started eating each other. Or at least threatening to. "Come on. And stay close, ok? Mr. Phil needs to introduce us first. Before the three of you go wild."

She got her two youngest out of their car seats while Evey climbed out of her booster. "What if they are cannibals, Mom? We don't know these people, after all. You've moved us clear across the world, where the cannibals are! We're doomed!"

"Evangeline Robin Carnes! That is enough, young lady."

Evey mimed eating her sisters, making the two younger girls squeal. Just as the front door of the house opened and bodies spilled out.

Lots of bodies.

Her own nerves had her gripping Evey's shoulder and swinging her youngest onto her hip. Emmy—there was never any holding her hand. It just didn't happen. "We can do this. Remember: this is our first day of our new adventure."

"Or our last day forever," Evy whispered, as the old dog finally made her way off the front step to limp toward Phil. *Nom, nom, nom.* They'll eat Emmy first!"

"Then it will be our last day together. Behave for the next five minutes, young lady. Or I'll clobber you."

Evey just shot her an angelic and wicked grin. Her children were monsters, but she loved them so much. Phil bent down and rubbed the dog's head gently. As his front yard filled with people. Lots of people in snow boots and winter coats.

There were four tall, extremely handsome men with broad shoulders and gorgeous faces, a few years younger than Glenna herself. There were four young women, who'd all stayed on the porch—every one of them redheaded. They all looked at Glenna —with faces a great deal like Robin's.

"Oh, my. They do look quite a bit like Robin, don't they?" she said before she thought it through. She could see various parts of Robin staring back at her.

Phil heard. "Very much so. The twins acted like she did, too. Pure hell on wheels. Don't be nervous. None of them bite, except the big guy there holding my granddaughter, Ivy. She's about five months or so older than your Emmy. He can be a bit cranky. Runs the hospital here in the county. A great doctor." Phil turned toward his family as a broad-shouldered young man stepped outside. "Listen up, crowd. I have something to say."

"When do you not, Dad?" one girl said, taunting, as two more boys tumbled outside, another dog at their heels. The house just kept spitting out *bodies*.

"Hush, Pandora, before I ground you." Phil held up his hand. "First, kids, I got great news. News we've been waiting for a very long time."

"What?" a woman said from next to a man with a sheriff's badge on his chest. She stepped closer, eyes on Glenna.

"I've found Robin. She's been living in Finley Creek for years." He held up a hand when the girls all exclaimed and threw questions at him. "She's going to visit us this summer. She has three kids, younger than Parker. Hush, no questions yet. I'm tired—we're all tired. It's been a long drive."

"Is she ok?" another woman asked. Her dark reddish-brown hair was the same color as Robin's and worn in a similar style. She even sounded like her aunt.

"She is. Had a few hard knocks, but she's going to be just fine. I hope she decides to stay around here. So you kids can get to know her again. Second, I have hired Mrs. Carnes here to be our housekeeper for a while, until she gets settled. Decides if Masterson is the place for her and her girls. Glenna's your aunt's closest friend and has agreed to live here on the place, with her three little girls. To help us all out since our numbers have grown so fast."

Glenna fought the nerves when everyone stared at her. Her hand tightened on Elly. Evey had already pulled her hand away to stare at Phil's family. Especially the youngest boy, who was staring at Glenna.

Glenna fought the urge to scoop her girls up and drive away fast.

She was better in one-on-one counseling situations than when facing an entire extended family of people staring at her. Evaluating her—and her girls.

Even if they didn't look that frightening.

Well, Phil's daughters' husbands did look a little frightening, actually.

"These are her little ones, Evangeline, Emmaline, and Eleanor. Everyone, these are my family. Parker and Patton, they are ten and fourteen. Next is Pete. He's seventeen, almost eighteen. Then my oldest son Phoenix is in Hollywood working for Rowland Bowles, of all things. After Phoenix is my Pandora. She's the strawberry-blonde. That's her husband Levi next to her. Their little guy is Griffen. Then there is Nate; he's the doctor, and my daughter Persephone. That's their daughter Ivy with Nate, and Perci has Poppy. Next to her is Philippa—she goes by Pip—and her husband, Matt. Matt's the vet in town. Pip is the real brains behind my ranch here, and she runs Matt's small place as well. That's their twin boys Davin and Daniel, and their newest Marlowe is in the carrier on her father's chest there. Finally, my oldest is married to the sheriff. That's my Phoebe and her husband Joel, and their daughter Aria. And this fluff ball is Liberty, the border collie. She's almost as old as Pete, so we just let her do whatever she wants. This little guy is Wally, and his sister is Winnie—we're not exactly sure if he's a dog or part goat. He'll eat just about anything. Winnie's a sweetheart, though, and tends to watch over Lib, and all the babies. Girls, don't worry about dinner. I've ordered pizza. Hopefully enough for everyone."

"Does everyone live *here?*" Emmy asked loudly. "The house is way too small."

Phil laughed, reaching for her hand. To Glenna's surprise, Emmy took his. "No, honey. We just like to get together a lot. My daughters and their husbands live other places. It's just me, Pete, Parker, and Patton living here now. And you three and your mommy."

One of the man's daughters stepped off the porch. She was taller than the rest and looked very much like Robin's little Becky. Her face was more rounded like Robin's, and her eyes shaped just like her aunt's. But the strawberry-blond hair was her father's. "Hi, I'm Pan. I bet you three will like to see your new rooms, right?"

The older two girls nodded. Elly clung to Glenna's shoulder suspiciously.

"You look like Aunt Robin." Evey had to point out. "But your hair is a lot lighter."

"Do I? I've seen pictures when Robin was little, so I guess I do." The woman looked more like her father, but the resemblance was there. Especially with the eyes. But the twins—they resembled Robin very strongly through the face and coloring. Three of Phil's daughters had the same hair as Robin. That was disconcerting, for some strange reason. Both disconcerting... and comforting. This was Robin's family. They would be ok here. "Dad, which rooms?"

"I was thinking Glenna would like Phoebe's room, and put the older girls in the twins' room, and little Elly in Phoenix's old room since it would be closest to her mother." He turned to Glenna. "The girls' rooms were all right across from each other. So they could squabble and slam doors at each other. You'll be able to be right across from them. There is also some attic space where Pan slept for years. It has access in the larger room, if you want to store some things up there or set up a private space for yourself. I'll do some moving around when Robin gets here if she wants to stay with us for a while."

"We don't want to be any trouble." It had sounded so practical when she'd first agreed to this, but now that they were actually there, it was starting to overwhelm her.

Sudden change had always freaked her out a little.

Glenna pulled the girls a little closer.

"You won't be. We're used to making things work in this house," one twin said. She wore scrubs. It was all that Glenna could see distinguished her from her identical sister. *They* looked the most like Robin, with the same copper-brown hair and features. They even had similar voices to their aunt. "It's rather something we're known for. I'm thrilled my dad has got some help now. He was running himself ragged, trying to be Superman."

"I also spoke with Travis. If there is any traveling to be done now, it'll be him or Levi. For the time being. We're going to rotate if we have to. So we can all be with our families more. And we're going to let Fletcher buy in."

"That's wonderful, Dad," the other twin said quietly. She passed him the little boy in her arms when the child reached for him. "Just wonderful."

"What about school? Where will we do our school?" Evey asked again, eyeing Phil with suspicion. She had been the most resistant to the move. She'd wanted Aunt Rory to bring the policemen she worked with to Boethe Street and make all the bad guys in her father's family just go away.

She hadn't seemed to realize that it just couldn't work that way.

"Well, the boys all do their school at the dining room table. I made that table myself when I first bought this house. It's nice and sturdy. Ever so often, I'll take it out and sand it and make it shiny again. I probably need to do it soon anyway. And make it bigger, to make room for everybody to have a spot at the table since there are so many babies now. Ivy here spilled paint all over the table one day. Not the washable kind either."

"You do *stuff?*"

"All kinds of stuff." He shifted his grandson and gave him a casual kiss on his head as the toddler's eyes drifted shut. Just that easily. As if he had held a million children. Maybe he had. "During the day, I go around the ranch doing all sorts of stuff. Sometimes I make fences. Sometimes I'm feeding the horses or the cows we have. Sometimes I'm going fishing, too. But that's after the work is done. What kind of stuff do you like to do?"

"I don't know. I haven't really thought about it. I do like books. Do you have a library here?"

"I certainly do. My niece Nikki works there. And she owns the bookstore. Plus, there are a lot of children's books we've collected over the years in a tote in the basement."

"What about T-ball? Do they have T-ball here?" Emmy asked, obviously wanting her share of his attention.

"Yes. We're signing Ivy up to play with the little kids this summer. Sign-ups will be in a month, then it'll start about a month after that. When the snow has hopefully stopped. If not, practices are inside the school gym."

"Ok. I think we can stay, then."

That was all it took, apparently.

Phil passed his now sleeping grandson to his older son. The teenager took the baby just as easily as his father had. "I want to get the boys on getting Glenna's things unloaded before the light sets."

"We'll help her and the girls figure this place out," one of his daughters said. Glenna looked at her closely—she had a hearing aid in one ear. Phil had told her his oldest, Phoebe, was deaf. "Glad you're back, Dad."

She hugged her father tightly. He kissed her on the

forehead.

"I'm glad to be home."

"I want all the answers about Robin later."

"I know. I can't wait to tell you all."

To her surprise, he turned to his sons-in-law and his three boys after the older boy returned without the toddler in his arms. Glenna assumed he'd laid the little boy down somewhere inside. "There are boxes in the truck. Let's get them into the study for now. They can be unpacked later."

"Let's get them inside before the sun goes down," one son-in-law said.

Just like that, five tall, strong men and three boys went to work while their wives carried all the babies inside.

There were a lot of babies.

This wasn't a scary place. This was just a *family*. Maybe it wasn't the kind of family she was used to—but it could be a good place for her and the girls to build the kind of roots they all needed.

It was going to take time, and take her putting herself out there to make those connections. That was going to be the hard part.

Glenna knew herself very well, after all.

Making friendships had always been difficult for her.

She didn't want it to be difficult for her daughters. She wanted them to have the confidence to make those connections. Lifelong ones. Unlike she had.

Glenna wanted her girls to feel like they *belonged* somewhere, more than anything. Safety and belonging—something she hadn't had much of herself.

She pulled in a deep breath, still feeling the chill in the air off the mountain. Fresh air. Clean air.

She was finally in a world where she didn't have to constantly look over her shoulder.

Glenna was going to make this work, somehow.

Six

IF IT WASN'T FOR HER BABY SLEEPING IN THE SMALL alcove fifteen feet from her bed, Phoebe Masterson would take out her hearing aid for the night.

Just so she could finally get some sleep. Sleeping next to Joel Masterson was like sleeping next to a freight train.

The man...just would not stop snoring. She knew her husband was completely exhausted, but wow.

The man was snoring worse than he ever had before. Phoebe almost swore the entire upstairs of their home had to be rattling. With the hearing aid in, she had almost sixty percent hearing in one ear. She needed it to hear her daughter in the middle of the night.

Joel's snoring was about to drive her insane.

He flopped over onto his back, his large, muscled body taking up far too much of her side of the bed. That, she didn't really mind. Sleeping pressed up against him was one of her all-time favorite things. She was surprised he hadn't woken the neighbors he was so loud tonight.

The nearest neighbors were his brother and her sister Perci almost a quarter of a mile away. She almost called Nate and held the phone up to Joel's face so Nate could find *something* to make his brother stop snoring somehow.

Before it drove Phoebe insane.

Joel flipped over again. The snoring stopped. One hard arm slipped around her waist. "Mmmm. Pretty smell. Woman. My woman. Caveman want my woman now."

Well, he was awake, then. She leaned up and kissed him lightly. "You should be sleeping."

"So should you. It's early. Don't you have to be at your dad's by nine today?"

Phoebe nodded, as worry filled her again. Her father was what had had her worried enough to not sleep in the first place.

Joel's snoring had just been an added…bonus. "Yes."

"You're worrying over something. Spill." Joel snuggled her close. Phoebe rested her head over his heart. Near the scars. It had been almost three years now.

One finger traced the ridges of flesh lightly. Remembering.

"Honey? Talk to me."

"I'm worried. About my father."

"And the fact that he just showed up tonight with a woman we've never met, moved her into his house, and she's now going to be taking over the primary care of the brothers you've basically helped raise?"

Talk about summing it up quickly. He'd nailed it. "Yes, something like that. She seems like a nice enough woman."

"Reserved. Kind of shy. Reminds me a bit of our Pip, actually. Same…expression in her eyes. And she's a very pretty woman."

Did he have to emphasize that last point like that? "What's that got to do with anything? What if she's a serial killer?"

He laughed lightly. Phoebe tweaked some of the light chest hair over his heart. Butthead. "She's not a serial killer. And she's pretty—I think that matters because your father has definitely noticed."

"What?" That hadn't even occurred to her. Glenna was only a few years or so older than Joel. Maybe even the same age. Or younger. And she had three little kids. The youngest wasn't even three yet. Surely she was too young for Phoebe's dad?

"Yes. I think your dad is attracted to her. Doesn't mean he'll act on it. And honey, she's not a serial killer. I called your father's business partner. Asked him if he knew her."

"And?"

"He said she's worked with his wife at a women's charity for a few years. Said Glenna's a nice lady who is a bit down on her luck right now, who is friends with Lacy Deane. She's not out to suck your father dry. I promise."

"Still...this is all so sudden."

"Well, sometimes a man sees a pretty girl, and his juices start to flow. And he'll do anything to get her where he can... get her."

Phoebe found herself on her back in a quarter of a second flat. With a gorgeous man looming over her with intent in his eyes. Ready to *get* her.

He should be far too tired for this. Her fingers flexed on the muscles of his arm. He felt like solid rock. Steady, perfect.

Her heart.

If she had lost him back when Rutherford had nearly killed him...

She hadn't. She had him now. He was right there, and she loved him so much. To lose him would destroy her. She finally understood how her mother's death had impacted her father. To lose the one you loved, to know your child had lost them, too...it would destroy her if she ever lost Joel.

"I don't know if he's ready," she said. "He loved my mother so much."

"I have no doubt that he did. Like my mom said when I asked her about Gerald after he started chasing her around everywhere...going through life alone is no way to go through life at all. Your dad has several good decades left in him. The boys will be grown and gone faster than he can blink. You girls are. Phoenix is. Pete only has a year left until he's eighteen. Maybe your dad needs someone, too."

"Maybe. I am still reserving judgment. I don't want her to hurt him."

"Whatever happens between them will be because it is meant to. Nothing we can do will stop that. Hurt or not."

"No. But..."

"Your father is a grown man, healthy, and not all that old. Let him figure this out for himself. He'll be ok. Now...baby still asleep?"

Phoebe checked, just as her husband did. "Yes."

"Good. Now...I got you all to myself." He whispered it close to her good ear. So she couldn't miss it. She shivered at what he meant, at what his hands were doing.

Phoebe laughed quietly and held her husband close.

Maybe she wouldn't clobber him after all.

But...she was going to reserve judgment about this house-keeper of her father's. Just to be on the safe side.

Seven

Phoenix Tyler disconnected the call from his sister Pandora and sank back onto the couch in the efficiency apartment that was *his*. He paid for it all by himself and took pride in that. He didn't know what he thought about what Pan had had to say. She called him every Thursday night. Like clockwork. Pan loved living by a schedule. Phoenix bet that drove her husband, Levi, insane.

It would Phoenix. He preferred to go with the flow more than Pan—or their sister Phoebe—ever had.

Pan had said everyone was doing ok. That their dad was going to semiretire from all of his traveling. Phoenix thought that was a good thing. He hadn't liked the idea of his father flying all over the place. Anything could have happened to him, and he still had Pete, Patton and Parker to take care of.

The thought that he could lose his father at any moment had acid twisting Phoenix's stomach. He stood, intending to grab himself a glass of milk if he had any. He usually ate cereal for breakfast—it was fast, and cheap, and L.A. wasn't exactly affordable. He should still have some good milk in the fridge.

His dad had brought a strange woman with three kids back from Texas with him to help out.

Phoenix didn't know what he thought about that. His father wasn't a stupid man. And Pan had spoken about finding their aunt. That their aunt knew this woman.

Still, what did they really know about her? She could be a con woman out to get what she could get. Phoenix had met a few of them in L.A. Women who were so damned mercenary they had dollar signs in their eyes when they looked at a rich man.

Phoenix definitely wasn't a rich man. He wasn't in L.A. to get rich anyway. He was there to learn, to create. To make something of himself. He'd first left Masterson with the director Rowland Bowles because it was a way out of Masterson County. But he liked what he did now.

He looked around at his studio apartment with his Murphy bed that he very rarely made. Only when he was having female company. He needed to clean the place up. He was starting to live like a pig.

His father would thump him on the back of the head if he saw how Phoenix was living right now. That had him bypassing the fridge and heading toward the sink. Where dirty dishes were piled up. He winced.

Yeah, he could do better than this.

As he cleaned his apartment, he wondered about the woman his father had just moved into the house without even asking his sisters and brothers about it first. She was going to be taking care of his younger brothers. Phoenix had questions.

He'd have to get them answered. Rowland was already making plans to return to Masterson County first thing in the morning to check on Hunter Clark's latest project—that Hunter was working on with Phoenix's cousin, Nikki.

Phoenix made a decision—he was going to talk Rowland

into taking him with him. He had some savings put back—he'd been wanting a bigger apartment and had needed a down payment—but this was worth the cost.

He wanted to check on his family for himself.

Eight

THE GIRLS HAD ENDED UP IN THE BED WITH HER IN the middle of the night. All three of them. Probably because they were scared in a new place. Emmy had somehow sprawled across Glenna's feet. Glenna had been aware of her child there all night, and Glenna hadn't wanted to kick her. She'd mostly just dozed.

She hadn't exactly slept well. That was for sure. She was up before the five thirty a.m. alarm could ring. She scooted Emmy up to the pillow next to her baby sister and covered her daughters with the quilt she suspected was hand made. There was a slight chill in the air she definitely wasn't used to. She looked back at the bed.

Her three little babies slept so peacefully. They were so beautiful.

Blond, green-eyed, and sweet. Most of the time. They had their wild moments, but she wouldn't trade a single one of those moments for anything in the world.

There was nothing she loved more than being a mother.

They had nowhere they had to be today. No errands to run

before she took them to a daycare to be watched over by people she didn't really know, no counseling sessions for her to oversee while the girls played in the playroom by themselves. All they had to do was get settled in their new—and temporary —home.

She wouldn't have them out until almost ten every night either.

They could have a normal kid bedtime again.

All she had to do was make this work. It wasn't intended to be permanent, just long enough for her to go through the process of licensing in Wyoming. *If* she decided Wyoming was where she wanted to stay. It was a chance at a different life for all of them.

She could go back to Finley Creek if she had to. But that was the last thing she wanted. With Lincoln's family always watching them—she just couldn't live like that any longer. It would mean selling her house, moving to another neighborhood. Hoping they didn't eventually find out where she and the girls were, constantly looking over her shoulder.

No. That wasn't the kind of life she wanted for herself either.

Glenna knew how to work. She'd been doing it since her first job at fourteen. She would make *this* work, too.

She could hear someone moving around in the hallway. There was a bathroom right outside her door. The house only had two bathrooms. One upstairs and one down.

From the time, she strongly suspected she knew just who it was out there. She wasn't quite ready to face him—especially not with bedhead and morning breath.

Not that that mattered, she didn't think. Why would he care if she was dressed in seriously unattractive yoga pants and a nightshirt?

If she looked like a forty-one-year-old working mom of three

—that was exactly what she was. He had hired her to help him with his house and his kids. That was it.

She had to remember that.

Dating was something that had never come easily to her. She had been too reserved for that all those years ago.

Until Lincoln had swooped into her world and gotten her so shaken up.

She had loved him. During the early years of their marriage. She would swear she did.

Of course, he had been gone a good portion of those years.

She had just gotten used to doing her own thing without him. She'd done her own thing for years and had grown up in the process.

Glenna wasn't proud of herself, but she hid. Waited until she heard Phil head downstairs. Then she rushed through her shower as fast as she could—she suspected there wasn't much hot water—and headed down the back stairs.

Into the kitchen.

Where Phil waited.

He was starting the coffee pot. "Good morning, how did you sleep?"

"Not great. The girls decided to climb on top of me all night. And they seriously wiggle. Elly has sharp little feet." The girls, she would just talk about the girls. That seemed like a safe enough topic to talk about with a man who had eight children and seven grandchildren.

He laughed. "I can say I am glad mine have outgrown that, though Parker still has some pretty bad nightmares at night. He'll camp out on the floor next to my bed sometimes. I always check to make sure I am not about to step on him in the mornings. He had some rough stuff happen when he was younger that has stuck with him."

"I can understand that." Glenna looked around the spotless,

if slightly dated, kitchen. There was, thankfully, a relatively new dishwasher. She abhorred doing dishes. The rest of the things a housekeeper did didn't bother her—she'd cleaned her way through college, after all—but dishes… Not her favorite chore. "What do I need to do first? Everything is clean in here."

"Food. Basically, just keep us fed, and we're good. And keep us in dry clothes. It can get cold and wet around here. Sometimes the boys and I go through two or three pairs of jeans a day, just doing the chores."

"I can do that." Should be simple. She knew how to cook, too. She'd waitressed and cooked for a few years on top of cleaning. Glenna knew how to work. She suspected her new boss did, too. "You, Parker, Pete, and Patton?"

"That's the usual crew. I have a few nephews who will stop by now and then—all redheaded and blue-eyed, so don't get upset if you see them wandering around, in and out—but for the most part, it's my three boys and me now."

"And me, and my three girls."

"Yep. There is plenty of food in the pantry and freezers. We keep it stocked year round. The girls put in a big garden every year, too. We tripled it after they married. They say they like home-canned food better, so they still do it here when it's time. I think they just like the tradition, doing it together. They like to make bread in the bread machine a few times a week for their brothers. Not that it lasts long. They've taught Patton how to use it, too. He's still learning, but he's getting better."

Glenna nodded, trying to make note of what he was saying. "Ok. Any specific times everyone likes to eat?"

"Breakfast at seven thirty. The boys and I handle the chores around six thirty, then they like to eat right after. Lunch is around noon and dinner six-thirty. If that doesn't work for you, we can rearrange things."

"No. I'm your housekeeper, I'll adjust if needed."

"Pete is finishing up outside now. He's usually up before I am. Drives me crazy, but he prefers the mornings. If you need anything just ask him. I'm heading out to tend the stock in the far barn. I'll be back in a bit. Take it easy today. Just feel your way around here. We Tylers really don't bite. I promise."

He squeezed her elbow in his hot hand. Glenna refused to let herself shiver.

To feel the fire that his touch shot through her.

She had *not* counted on being attracted to him when she accepted his offer.

This…was crazy.

Not what she anticipated at all.

First chance she got, she was calling Rory. See what her friend thought. Rory was far more experienced with men than Glenna.

Not that it took much, but Rory at least *dated* occasionally.

Glenna wasn't certain she wanted to tell Robin how Robin's brother-in-law made her *feel* either.

Glenna just nodded, not sure what else to say. After he left through the back door of the kitchen, she spent a few minutes just poking around, checking to see what staples were in the cabinets and that sort of thing. She'd never used home-canned vegetables in her life. There was even homemade apple butter in there.

She just tried to figure out what to do next.

Glenna was captain of the ship today.

By the time she was finished, three boys were looking at her —and her three girls were standing there in pajamas, wondering what they were all supposed to do next.

"I may be a few minutes late on breakfast, boys. I hope that's not a problem."

Parker sent her a wicked smile, looking very much like Robin. "No problem. If breakfast is late, school is late. I can handle that."

Glenna laughed. He was a wicked one, all right. "I suppose you can."

She'd thought to give her girls a few days off from school to get acclimated, but she changed her mind. A small, unhurried lesson or two today wouldn't hurt. Begin as they meant to go on, after all.

It might help them in the long run if she established the routine from the very beginning.

She could do this.

It was just breakfast.

For eight people. She could do this. She'd just pretend Robin and her kids were there—and then add a bit more. Just in case.

"What do you boys usually eat for breakfast?" Please don't say bacon and eggs and pancakes and the whole spread. She wasn't up for that at all.

But Glenna could make this work.

If not, she would find a job in Masterson and rent a house, and build a life here for her daughters. She was getting rental money from her house in Finley Creek, too. That would help. Cost of living in Masterson was probably a lot less than in Finley Creek. She could make things work.

She could figure it out. If this didn't work out, she'd *make* it happen somehow.

"The girls usually just make a big pot of oatmeal or a bunch of scrambled eggs. Nothing too complicated. Everyone is usually too busy for that. Then we get on our school, once Phoebe gets here. Tend to get it out of the way early so we can do chores and then just hang out," Pete said. He gave her a reassuring smile, very much like his father's. "We'll figure this out as we go along. Tylers are used to making do, you know. It's kind of what we do."

"Thanks." She shouldn't freak out over feeding a bunch of

kids. She was going to have to gain control of herself a bit more.

This wasn't healthy. Freaking and second guessing. She'd been this way ever since that day. When Lincoln had been killed right in front of her. She'd seem him skid out when another driver ran a red light. Knew he was going to be hurt.

She'd swerved out of the way, barely missing being hit herself. Her and the girls. All three of the girls had been in their car seats behind her.

It had been one of the worst days of her life. Knowing he was probably dying and not being able to leave the girls to get to him. To help somehow.

He had fathered her children. He had died in front of her. No matter what had happened between them, that was something she could never forget.

Glenna shoved the memories away as she opened the fridge. She'd seen a big bowl of fresh eggs just sitting there. She suspected they were as fresh from the farm as they could get. She'd probably have to wash them first. Really, really well.

She had no idea how to deal with fresh eggs at all.

Well, she could just google it.

She could handle this. Scrambled eggs. Four eggs per kid, though her girls would eat less than that. If it didn't look like enough, she'd make a few pieces of toast each. That would work today. There was a big jug of orange juice and a carton of milk.

She had breakfast handled.

She'd figure out lunch when the time came. Soup or stew or something that would stretch, if needed. The bread machine was right there. She had time to make dinner rolls.

And—heaven help her—dinner.

"How many people are usually here for dinner?" she asked. She'd have to start preparing things early.

Pete frowned, a look of sadness going through his blue eyes that was unexpected. "It's been just us and Dad for a while now. Unless we go to one of our sisters', or they all come over here. But they bring food when they do that, and Dad grills something or throws in a roast. He's a decent cook. Of course, he's in Texas a lot now. But he promised that was going to change."

From the look on the young man's face, Glenna suspected she knew why he had made that promise. "I'm not entirely certain what he does in Texas."

"He's involved in a specialty cattle breed development project. Him and Levi—that's my brother-in-law, the one with Pan—and Mr. Worthington-Deane from Finley Creek."

"I've met Travis. I'm good friends with his wife. I've babysat his daughter a few times."

"But Dad said he's not going to travel as much now. He says he wants to be here with us boys and working the ranch. He promised." And she sensed that mattered to this boy. He looked like a full-grown man, now, but he was still young. "Dad really tries to keep his promises. Especially to us."

"That's good." She didn't ask about his mother. Robin had told her about her sister Rebecca before. And Glenna had seen the photos of the woman who looked very much like her daughters—and her niece, little Becky.

She had seen the love on the woman's face in those photos, surrounded by her eight children. And the husband who had loved her. A pang of empathy went through her for all of them. They hadn't deserved to lose her that way.

She bet Phil had been a good husband. Kind and loving to his wife. The kind Glenna hadn't had. For some women, that just wasn't really written in the cards.

Parker eyed her suspiciously. He hadn't taken to having her —or the girls—in his space that openly. He was about a year or so older than Robin's boys and looked very much like them, only with strawberry-blond hair instead of their burnished brown.

In the meantime, Glenna wasn't entirely certain how to relate to him. He didn't trust her. And she suspected he didn't want her in his space, replacing the women who had cared for him his entire life. That would make sense to her, if she was in his place. "Are you really hungry, Parker?"

He nodded. Eyed her suspiciously again. "We were in the movies, you know."

"Were you?"

"Yes. Rowland Bowles, the Hollywood director, put me in his movie. My brothers and sisters and some of my cousins, too. Nikki got a really funny part with a funny helmet and everything. My dad wasn't in it, but they made the movie in our front yard. And Levi's. Then Rowland took Phoenix with him when he left."

"I see." She didn't, but...he was trying to rattle her. She just knew it.

He nodded. Still eyeing her suspiciously. She had her work cut out with this one. "Yes. I was really good. I'm going to Hollywood one day to be in more movies. Have you ever been in movies?"

She suspected if she said no, she'd go down a notch in his estimation. But... "Once. I was in a crowd scene and got to point at a cartoon elephant walking down the street. We have a film studio in Finley Creek. They make a lot of kids' movies. It was fun."

Still the suspicion. "I did so good I got a bigger part. I'm in the big scene at the end of the movie, too. My character almost *died*. And I was fifteen thousand years old."

"And where can I watch this movie? I've never known a real movie star before."

"It's not out yet. There was a lot of special effects that got messed up and had to be fixed. It takes time. But it'll come out soon." He was apparently very wise on the making of movies.

"I'm looking forward to watching it. I can't wait to see you in a movie."

The eggs were ready. Within moments, she had six kids surrounding her at the table.

His on one side of the table. Hers on the other. Like a war ready to begin?

The younger five kept eyeing each other suspiciously. The oldest was clearly used to being in charge of his brothers.

Just as she was finishing getting the girls' plates ready, the back door opened.

And there *he* was, looking like a cowboy. Phil wasn't the most physically beautiful man she had ever seen, but he was very, very attractive. In that rugged western way that some men had.

She'd seen photos of him when he was younger, on the walls of his house. He'd looked good then. But some men got so much better with age.

Her cheeks heated when the thought struck her that *this* was one of them.

His shoulders were broad, his chest looked firm and hard, and his face was only a little weathered by time. His hair was a mix of gray and lighter red that was highly attractive.

For the first time, she realized something she hadn't before —he wasn't that much older than she was.

Eight or nine years maybe.

He'd just gotten started having his children young—while she had waited until her thirties to even marry.

He was a very attractive man.

Glenna wasn't in the market for a man. No matter what. She was going to keep reminding herself of that as long as she had to.

No. It wasn't going to happen. That would just mess everything up for them right now. She wouldn't do that to her girls. She just wouldn't.

Breakfast went quickly, and then Phil was gone again. Back out to handle calves or something.

She was just finishing up breakfast with Elly—her youngest was a bit picky and slow—when the back door opened and one of Phil's daughters stepped in, a look of determination on her face that said she was a woman on a mission.

Nine

GLENNA HAD TO ADMIT THAT, OF ALL OF PHIL'S daughters, she found *this* one the most intimidating.

Not because of her hearing issues but because Phoebe was the oldest. She'd naturally taken over her mother's role with Phil's family after his wife's death. Phoebe was probably used to being in charge, even though she didn't live here any longer. She was bound to feel a bit displaced, having someone else in her father's home, caring for her younger brothers.

Even as a temporary housekeeper.

She watched as the woman lowered her daughter's carrier to the table. "Can I help you grab anything? It is cold out there."

"I got it, thank you." Phoebe Tyler Masterson was very small —just like Robin. She had to be barely five one or so. Once again, just like Robin. Glenna thought she was around twenty-eight or so and very beautiful. She sent Glenna a smile.

Just like Robin's.

It didn't do a thing to help Glenna relax.

This woman was married to the sheriff, after all.

Thanks to Lincoln's absurd fear of the police—which she

now knew was because of his drug use, and his family's—that had Glenna more than a little nervous. He had conditioned her well during their years together.

Just how much of a stranglehold he'd had on her life became clearer the longer time passed.

The baby laughed, drawing Glenna's attention.

"The baby is gorgeous. But I'm afraid I don't remember which baby is with which…"

"This is Aria. I am Phoebe, by the way," Phil's daughter said, taking off her coat and handing it to Parker, who hung it on a peg by the back door. "We can be a bit confusing. Or so my husband has told me. Would you like to hold her?"

"I would love to. My baby is almost three going on eighty." Glenna took the little girl and held her.

"Are you settling in well?"

"I…think so." She knew exactly what Phoebe was doing. Checking her out. "I still have to figure out lunch and dinner and get the girls started on school, but…no time like the present to build our routine."

The woman was on a mission.

That mission was Glenna.

$\mathcal{T}_{\varepsilon n}$

Glenna had figured her out. Phoebe would give her that.

Glenna was a quiet woman. The opposite of how Phoebe's mother had been. Glenna was more like Pip. Her mother had been much more like the fierier Perci.

Glenna had a soothing manner about her that Phoebe probably would have liked if they had met anywhere else but her father's front yard the night before. She probably *would* like Glenna.

Phoebe was reserving judgment.

She was a bit distrustful where strangers were concerned. It had taken her a while to trust Joel, too.

Phoebe settled in for the day. She wasn't going anywhere.

Glenna's daughters were total hellions that reminded Phoebe of Perci, Pan, and Pip as children. Phoebe had always had to ride herd on them to keep them out of trouble.

Parker seemed to enjoy having children around to play with, but he took off to his bedroom after a while. Said there were too many girls around. Patton had choir practice, and Pete had driven him in to town. Pete was flirting around with a girl right now, and took every opportunity to go to town to see if he could run into her.

Phoebe busied herself by helping Glenna prepare a pot roast for dinner.

Glenna seemed...competent. Nice.

A little shy. Phoebe hadn't really expected that, for some reason.

Not exactly like someone trying to sink her claws into Phoebe's innocent, overly trusting father. Phoebe smirked to herself as she imagined her father's response if she ever called him that out loud.

Her father wasn't innocent and unknowing and vulnerable —not even for one moment.

He was strong, healthy, and...needed. Very, very needed. He'd had a heart attack after her mother's death, but the underlying cause had been found and surgically corrected shortly after.

It had terrified them all, reminding them how quickly someone could be lost. Phoebe would *never* forget how tenuous life could be. How quickly someone you loved could be just gone in an instant.

It was after that scary night when Phoebe had taken over in so many ways. And had organized her sisters into very efficient little lieutenants to do her bidding.

They had marched to her orders like good little soldiers until they hadn't needed to any longer.

All of that was over now thankfully.

But old habits died hard.

Her father was healthy. He was relatively young. And he had children to raise.

She knew exactly how hard that was, and how much work the ranch was. He'd had to hire two of her younger cousins part-time to help replace Pip. Her sister still helped when she could, but Pip had three children and her own plans for life now.

Phoebe falling for Joel had changed everything for everyone. In a good way. But it had definitely meant change.

She probably would have still met Joel. She'd come to that realization a few years ago, watching the way her sisters had circled around with his brothers. With the way his brother Nate and her sister Perci had been with each other, and the way Pan had been hired by Levi as his housekeeper...meeting Joel would have been inevitable.

Change was inevitable.

Just *how* it had happened, had been totally random.

Phoebe was starting to accept that she couldn't control everything anymore. But she knew herself well—she was good at being the one in charge.

But...she really couldn't be in charge at her dad's. Not anymore. He and the boys had to do what was best for *them*. Regardless of what she thought about it.

What she thought about a stranger in her mother's kitchen.

She tried to tell herself that as Glenna held her own youngest close and rocked the girl until she was sound asleep. The older girls were in the family room watching an educational program for a few minutes while Glenna tended her youngest and Phoebe took care of Aria. "Are the girls settling in ok?"

Glenna nodded. "I think so. I have always homeschooled. So thankfully, we don't have to change that routine. When I was working second shift at the women's charity, the girls came with me. And we did their school during slow times. I'm glad for a more normal routine. They want to do their school tomorrow when Parker does. They idolize him."

"He probably likes that. I think, as the baby of the family—he's also the youngest cousin—he was feeling a bit invisible. The movie made him feel important. And he likes it."

"He's wonderful. They all are. Your father has helped me out so much letting us stay here."

"He needed the help, too."

"That's what he said. But he could have hired someone local. He…I think he only hired me to help Robin out. And because Lacy Deane asked him to. Lacy and Robin were worried about me."

Robin. Phoebe hadn't seen her since Phoebe was seven years old. "How long have you known Robin?"

"Thirteen years. She was there with me for every one of my girls' births. Evey's middle name is Robin. Robin and her kids, and our friend Rory—they are my family. I have always been able to count on them."

She meant it.

Phoebe knew she was pushing when she asked the question that was burning in her mind. "And the girls' father? Where is he?"

Eleven

PHIL HAD SEEN HIS DAUGHTER'S LITTLE SUV ON HIS walk down from the upper barn. He had suspected his oldest would show up to question him today. He had seen Phoebe watching him and Glenna the night before.

His eldest child knew her old man very well. And Phoebe liked to be in charge.

Now his favorite little dictator—who could give Joel a good run for his money at natural interrogation ability—was on the attack.

He slipped into the mudroom at the rear of the house and chucked off his boots. And the wet socks. Snow had gotten in when it shouldn't have. He'd have to grab a new pair in town.

He didn't have to worry any longer about juggling funds enough to grab a pair of new boots whenever he needed them. Not like they had for a while there after the medical bills had nearly destroyed every sense of stability he and Becky had worked so long to achieve.

But that was over now.

His younger kids would have better than his eldest had.

He wished it wasn't so, wished he'd been able to give the

five older kids the same as the younger three, but Phil was also pretty damned philosophical about it. God hadn't given him anything Phil couldn't handle.

Except for losing Becky. Almost losing all the girls at one point or another. Those had been the darkest days of his life.

He would never forget the gnawing fear that he had felt waiting on word if his Perci would survive the bullet that had nearly torn her liver in half. But she was healthy and strong and helping her husband run the hospital that her mother-in-law had built years ago.

Already talking about having a third child to join the other two.

His girls were happy, with men who loved them, with children who would grow up to be happy and loved as well.

If there was one thing Tylers were good at, it was loving each other. If he managed nothing else in this world worth remembering, his kids knew he loved them. Each and every one.

He couldn't think of a better legacy than that.

He grabbed a pair of dry socks out of his bin in the laundry room—each person had a special bin for underclothes where they were in easy reach. Wyoming winters—and springs—were wet and damned cold, after all. It was a system Becky had figured out long ago.

Phil laughed quietly to himself when he saw that someone had marked out Pip's, Pan's, and Phoenix's names from their old wooden bins on the rack. In childish letters were Evey, Emmy, and Elly. Elly's was on the bottom where the little one could best reach. She was still a little too young to understand the system, but she was a part of it now.

It would be nice to have a houseful of kids again.

He'd missed it.

Far more than he wanted to admit. Since his girls had married and all left within months of each other.

Followed by Phoenix.

He was worried about that oldest boy of his. Phil would freely admit that.

He just wanted his son to make it through the ghosts still haunting him.

It wasn't Phoenix's fault his mother had died in that wreck. Everyone knew that now. He just wished Phoenix understood that Phil had never doubted him.

Phil slipped his socks on and stepped into the rear of the kitchen just as he heard his daughter ask the question he knew had been on everyone's mind before. "And the girls' father? Where is he?"

Phil looked to where Glenna sat in the old rocker that someone had put in the corner of the kitchen years ago. When they'd needed an extra chair at the table for whoever was staying with them at the time. It might have been his niece, Maggie. Or little Charlotte Talley when she'd stayed with them when she'd been eighteen, for a while.

That rocker had a place of honor in the kitchen.

Now Glenna sat in it, rocking her two-year-old. "He... died. Two years or so ago. Elly was not quite four months. We had just signed divorce papers at the time, were on the way to the attorneys' office for the final meeting when his motorcycle was struck. The girls and I saw it happen, and were almost hit ourselves. My childcare had canceled the last minute."

"I'm sorry," Phil said. Both women had known he was there. Glenna had looked up and met his eyes.

She nodded. "Thank you. He had a drug problem. I found out about what he was doing, and we tried to work through it. It spiraled from there."

He doubted it was as simple as she made it out to be. There was a load of hurt in those big green eyes of hers.

"What made you leave Finley Creek?" Phoebe could push,

could be a bit on the stubborn side. She'd gotten it from her mother.

"I know what you're asking," Glenna said. She sent Phoebe a significant look. His daughter smiled, completely unrepentant.

Instead of snapping something back, Glenna laughed lightly. "You're good. Remind me of Charlotte. Only she's much, much louder at getting what she wants."

"That's definitely her." Phoebe looked at him. "Glenna is a friend of Charlotte's, too. Did you know that?"

"I didn't."

Glenna looked at Phoebe. "My ex's family...has a dim understanding of boundaries. Lincoln didn't have a great support system. He had a violent juvenile record I wasn't aware of when we met and married. That is something his three brothers have continued on their own. I'm not sure one or two of them aren't in prison right now. At least one usually is. They started harassing me, wanting money. I talked it over with my closest friends. My leaving town quickly was my best option. When your father offered me this position, I took it. I...want my girls to grow up in a place where they don't have to live in fear of family they have never met. Lincoln was adamant that they not interact with his mother or his brothers. Lincoln's mother was high one day last week. She showed up at our homeschool co-op. Came right into the toddler group and tried to walk out with Elly. Told the teachers that she had grandparents' rights and I couldn't stop her. A friend saw what happened, realized something suspicious was going on with her, and recognized my daughter. He stopped them before they could get Elly to the car. That was the deciding incident. I was going to press charges, but was told they would be pled down to almost nothing. And...they lived three blocks away from us. I just didn't feel the girls were safe there any longer."

Phoebe gasped and tightened her arms around Aria.

Phil bit back his own curse. Now he understood how a college-educated woman would give up a career as a counselor to come wash his dishes and fold his socks, even temporarily.

Fear.

He'd known she'd had something going on, but he'd just wanted to help.

He was immensely glad he had.

"Will they show up here?" Phoebe asked.

"No. None of them have a car or money for plane tickets. They used public transit mostly. And all three of his brothers are terrified of violating parole. His mother—she won't bother now. I don't think. I just...the girls started being afraid. At the homeschool co-op, which they'd once loved. At W4HAV where I worked. Just everywhere. Robin and Rory—she's our other good friend—they wanted me to leave a while ago. I just... didn't know where to go. And with Robin coming up here soon...and your offer...I...it just felt right."

"Good. You are welcome here as long as you need to be here." He leaned down and cupped her cheeks. Right there in front of Ms. Nosy-Butt Phoebe Kate. He just ignored the instinctive flinch away. He suspected he knew how Glenna's marriage had been now. "I'll take care of you. Keep you safe right here. If you'll let me."

"Thank you. But I need to figure out how to take care of *me* again. You...thank you. I really mean that. You are showing my girls that not all men are the nightmare that their father turned out to be. Emmy and Evey...they remember bits and pieces of him. None of it good. I want to show them a different kind of life. That's all I want in the world." The last was said in a whisper that almost broke his heart. "For my girls to feel safe again."

Twelve

PHOEBE WAS ABOUT READY TO CRY, JUST AT THE emotion she felt swirling between the two.

Wow.

They probably didn't see it at all either.

There was a look in her father's eyes that tightened Phoebe's stomach, and it was matched by a softly hesitant look in Glenna's.

Connection.

Phoebe could almost feel a sizzle between them.

There was a connection there. One she definitely hadn't been expecting to see. But at least her doubts about Glenna had somewhat subsided.

Glenna seemed genuine. And when she looked down at her daughter, still sleeping in her arms, Phoebe understood her.

There wasn't anything she wouldn't do for Aria.

If that meant packing her baby up and moving clear across the country so Aria could grow up with love and not fear, well, Phoebe would do it. In an instant.

Leave everything else she loved behind. Including her family, if that was what it took.

For her child, a mother would do anything.

She saw that knowledge in Glenna's face.

Of course, a father would do the same.

Her own was lifting little Elly from Glenna's arms. The other woman stood—for the first time, Phoebe realized there was only about a dozen years or so between herself and Glenna. Her father had been almost twenty-three when Phoebe had been born.

So very young.

He was still relatively young. Working himself day and night, taking care of the boys, too. And then going to bed alone. She knew how lonely a cold bed could feel.

Phoebe didn't want him spending his life alone. Phoebe didn't.

And the way he was looking at Glenna...well...

She would do whatever she could to help the older woman feel at home here. To know she didn't have to live in fear either.

To know someone had tried to take your child, had almost succeeded—that had to be utterly terrifying.

Horribly terrifying. Just like it had been when Pan had been abducted, and then Perci a short time later. Phoebe had had her family to help her through it.

Glenna didn't seem to have many people at all.

Well, she was in Tyler country now.

Phoebe stood. She'd put her own baby down for her nap in the playpen her father kept in the living room now. And then she'd help get the living room cleaned up and set the table. Get dinner prep ready. Help where she could, before getting the boys started on their school for the day.

Joel was working late tonight—traffic detail at the high school. She would text him and let him know where she was going to spend dinner.

She was going to enjoy tonight with her father and brothers. And just see how Glenna fit with all of them.

Phoebe had just returned to the kitchen when the back door opened.

A tall man stood there. And he was a man. Not a boy. He was twenty-two now. The same age her father had been when she had been born. He had filled out in the year since he had last been home.

Was beautiful to look at.

Her brother had been a late bloomer. That was for sure.

A rush of love so strong nearly bowled her over. This was her baby brother, and she loved him. And he was *home*. "Phoenix!"

He opened his arms. "Phoebe. Come here, shrimp."

Just like that, she was hugging the brother she hadn't seen in far, far too long. "What are you doing here? We would come to the airport and gotten you…"

"I rode in with Rowland. He is staying with Pan and Levi tonight. He's trying to talk to Levi about filming on the ranch again." Phoenix hugged her back, but Phoebe hadn't missed the slight hesitation. It was always there whenever he was with them now. "Hunter is in town working on the script with Nikki. They're giving off a very do-not-disturb vibe. And Rowland gives Hunter whatever Hunter wants."

Phoebe stepped back, as her father pulled her brother close. Hugged him tight.

It had been hardest on their father, Phoenix leaving.

They had struggled together after her mother died, her father and Phoenix. Before that, Phoenix had wanted to live up to their father's expectations of what a Tyler should be. Ridiculous, of course. All her father had wanted was for Phoenix to have personal responsibility and accountability. And honor.

And to be happy.

She studied her brother again as he hugged their father just as tightly. Then Phoenix stepped back.

There was a maturity about her brother that hadn't been there before.

But the hurt was still there in the eyes so like her own.

Thirteen

PHOENIX HAD STAYED FOR DINNER, GETTING introduced to Glenna and the girls. He didn't say much more than hello. Or even give them more details about why he was in town. Hunter Louis Clark, the biggest actor in Hollywood right now was in town.

To work with Phil's niece Nikki on a documentary. Of the hells *Phil's* daughters had gone through three years ago. The entire idea of the project gave Phil a bit of a sour stomach. He didn't want to focus on those days for even a moment. But Rowland Bowles had saved his niece Nikki's life during those days, and had saved Pip and Perci and Matt's, too.

Phil owed him something for that. And Bowles had promised to do the documentary with class. The girls had agreed to it—but only if Nikki was in charge of it.

Hunter Louis Clark was currently—and secretly—holed up in an apartment over Nikki's bookstore. Working with Phil's far-too-innocent twenty-four-year-old niece. For hours.

Alone.

Phil definitely wasn't certain how he thought about that.

But Phoenix had assured him Clark was a professional. And wouldn't dare do anything he shouldn't with Nikki.

If he did, well, Phil had nephews ready to step in and reeducate Hunter on how things should go with a Tyler girl.

Phil actually *liked* Hunter. He had met the young man before —when Hunter had stepped in and helped save Phil's daughter Pandora when she'd gotten into trouble, too.

Pan considered the man a friend. They all trusted him.

The story of the Tylers of Masterson County would eventually be filmed and told. Phil wasn't certain how he felt about that.

It was just something else he had to think about as Phoenix took off back to L.A., and Glenna and the girls settled in more. The days got a bit easier—on all of them—as the week passed.

Some of the fear and tension in Glenna's eyes faded a bit.

That was exactly what Phil had wanted to see.

He thought about his housekeeper as he finished the repairs to the main barn door that had to be made before the next wave of snow came in. And just wondered what he'd have to do to replace that fear completely.

Phil would admit it to himself—he spent a lot of his free time thinking about that beautiful woman in the middle of his house now.

She was about all he could think about.

But what he was going to do about her—well, Phil hadn't figured that part out yet at all.

MC

GLENNA WAS at the stove when the door opened again and a half-frozen man stepped inside. She had coffee waiting for him.

He liked it when he spent more than a few minutes outside.

In the week she'd been his housekeeper, she'd realized that.

Phil was a man of simple needs. Food, dry clean clothing, coffee. And his kids. The man lived for time with his kids.

And…after the first day or so when her girls were still getting acclimated, he'd started including them.

Elly took to him the fastest. She lifted her arms for him to carry her every chance she could.

At first, it had made Glenna nervous. Until she'd realized what it was—Phil's grandchildren did the same to him every chance *they* could. The twins—Pip and Matt's oldest children—were only about ten months or so younger than Elly. But they were good-sized boys, who probably outweighed her little girl.

Elly wanted the same attention they got.

Phil was happy to oblige.

Emmy was next, but mostly because Phil's granddaughter Ivy did.

Evey was the holdout. Just like Glenna had known she would be. Patton was the one Evey seemed to connect with the most, even though he was far quieter than she was. It had to do with a shared love of books, Glenna thought.

Parker was the one who surprised her most.

Until she'd put it together. He missed being at the center of feminine attention like he'd probably had with his older sisters before they'd moved out.

He wanted *Glenna's* attention whenever he could manage it. Even if it meant bickering with Evey to get it.

But they were settling into a good rhythm. A good routine.

It was her attraction for the boys' father that was really disconcerting her. No matter what she told herself. It just wasn't going away. As he stepped closer and took the thermos of coffee from her, Glenna had to face the truth.

She somehow doubted it was going to go away anytime soon. She was going to just have to find a way to deal with it. Before she did something she'd regret.

"Thanks. I'm going to get back out there. I saw Phoebe pull in the drive a moment ago, too. I'll be back in to see how she's doing in just a few."

Glenna just nodded like an idiot. And watched him walk away.

Fourteen

PHOEBE HADN'T BEEN SO EXHAUSTED IN HER ENTIRE life. The baby had been up all night, and Joel had been called in to help an elderly woman near Phoebe's cousin Nikki's bookstore when she thought she saw a prowler. She had no clue how her mother had managed eight children. Especially the twins.

One child was absolutely exhausting her.

Phoebe told her daughter that, marveling again at how absolutely beautiful her baby was. She had Joel's smile. Wicked and mischievous. Aria lifted her foot to her mouth and tried to chew on the tiny boot.

"That won't taste very good," Phoebe warned Aria as she carried her inside her father's house as quickly as she could. Pete had a big project due in his co-op speech class. She was there to help him. Glenna had taken over the house chores, but Phoebe was still responsible for seeing that her brothers were homeschooled properly.

It was a massive undertaking, but one she had been doing for years. She had everything planned out by grade now.

She just…really needed a nap somehow.

Glenna was in the kitchen, taking a large pan of what looked to be meatballs out of the oven. She smiled when Phoebe walked in. "Good morning."

"You're hard at work." And looked super-energic. Phoebe fought the envy.

"Yes. For the first time since we got here, all three girls slept in their own beds. I've forgotten what that's like." Glenna studied her for a moment. "You look exhausted."

"I am." Far more than she was ready to admit aloud.

Glenna sat the pan on the stove and pulled off the oven mitts. "Let me help you with her."

"Thank you. She's teething, and we were up all night."

"I remember those days. I remember crying to Robin how I just couldn't do it any longer. I had a bit of postpartum after Evangeline. Lasted about three months. Then she started teething at five months. I don't really think I've slept a full night since—until last night. There are still some biscuits and gravy left. Have you eaten?"

Phoebe just shook her head. "I couldn't. I had a bit of an upset stomach, and I was so tired I didn't have time…"

Glenna patted her on the shoulder. "Sit, I'll get you something to eat. The kids are cleaning up their rooms now, and getting their school books. You have a few minutes."

They had figured out a routine for the homeschooling that was working well. Glenna gave her girls their instructions and got them started on whatever they needed to do—she was project-oriented, Phoebe had noticed. And that worked well for the oldest, with the middle girl participating as much as she was able, as she was still a bit too young for full homeschool yet. Glenna worked on the basics with the youngest girl when she could throughout the day. Singing songs and playing counting games, that kind of thing.

That left the other side of the dining room table for Parker and Patton and Pete, with Phoebe. It was a similar routine she'd worked out with Pip years ago, when Pip would take the younger two boys and Phoebe would work with Pete. School was more of a struggle for Pete than Patton or Parker. She had had to devote a great deal of time to him at first.

It was working out well with Glenna. She wasn't overstepping, but she wasn't timid about doing her job either.

She just sort of...blended in. Like she had always been there.

It was strange to see another woman in her mother's place in the kitchen though.

It had been different when it had been Pan doing the cooking and the cleaning. Or one of the twins.

But now...it was Glenna and her girls running around everywhere.

Phoebe still didn't know how that made her feel.

Fifteen

PHOEBE DIDN'T JUST LOOK EXHAUSTED. THE younger woman looked downright green. Glenna seriously hoped Phoebe wasn't coming down with something—not just because if she was, the entire household would probably catch it, but because taking care of an infant when you were ill was just not fun. And a lot of work.

"Why don't you take it easy this morning? I can help the boys with their school. I've already got half of dinner prepared to go into the slow cooker. I'll watch the baby. You curl up somewhere and take a nap."

Phoebe stared at her for a moment, a considering look in her eyes.

Glenna suspected this Tyler was very stubborn and probably a bit hard on herself, too. And...Phoebe liked being in charge. Finally, the woman slumped almost in defeat. "It gets easier, right?"

Glenna shook her head, then made sure to face Phoebe fully when she spoke. Parker had told her early on that that was very important, so Phoebe could hear her. He took his role as protector of his four older sisters very seriously, that child.

Being a brother, he'd told her, came with obligations. "It gets *different*, the older they get."

"Joel is called out at all hours. Most of the time, it's not a problem, but lately, I'm utterly exhausted."

"I remember those days. If I hadn't had Robin and Rory to help me, I don't know what I would have done. I can help, Phoebe. Just take a break. Besides, I am not *ever* having another one. I can use the cuddle time. You blink, and they are seven and too cool to want anything to do with you. Or almost three and telling you no more diapies, Mommy. Which...*that* I am seriously thankful for, but..."

"Yes. I don't know how Parker is ten. My mother struggled a bit physically after she had him. It was a difficult birth, and she had a hysterectomy right after. I helped out as much as I could with him. Now he's almost as tall as I am and sure he knows everything. And he's going to be a big movie star, you know?"

Glenna nodded. She had been informed of Parker's dreams right away. "So I've heard."

"He's not the baby he once was. But always with him, there were other people to help. Now, now I am so sure I won't hear her that I think I may be freaking out a bit at night. Especially since Joel needs to sleep, too. And I want to make sure he does."

Glenna stepped closer to the table and unfastened the baby from her carrier. The little one smiled at her. Glenna smiled back, instantly charmed. "Is there someone who can help you for a week or so? It sounds to me like you're hypervigilant right now, and need a break to reset."

Phoebe was probably holding herself to some ridiculously high new mother standards—and it had been going on for months.

Glenna had done that, too.

But whereas Phoebe's husband was legitimately unable to help her at night thanks to his job, Lincoln had just told Glenna that she had wanted the babies—it was her job to tend to them. The instant she'd told Rory that, the other woman had packed a bag and stayed for three weeks. With each baby. And then whenever she'd thought Glenna needed a break.

Rory had told Lincoln off several times, too.

Lincoln hadn't liked it, but Rory had scared him, being married to a cop with the TSP at the time. Having her in his house…had scared him into behaving.

Not into being a better father, though.

She wouldn't have made it through without Rory and Robin.

"All of my sisters have their own kids. And Rhea…well, she's busy with Gerald. He's a bit of a handful. She'd probably help, though. All I have to do is ask. But while I love my mother-in-law immensely…"

"You want to do it on your own." Glenna pulled Aria up to her shoulder, where the baby could chew happily. She'd been through teething enough to know exactly what to do. "And you can. You just have to find a way to get creative."

"What do you mean?"

"I mean, you sleep when you can. And forgive yourself when you need to take a minute or two for yourself. And don't be afraid to ask for help from those of us who've been in the trenches. Even for a day or two. You can't run yourself down— trust me: it's way too hard to get back up. There is an army of women out there who have been where you are. Time to activate it."

She was definitely a prideful one, this eldest daughter of Phil's.

Glenna could understand that. She knew exactly how exhausting it could be. And from what she'd observed, Phoebe was doing just fine. She just needed a little extra boost.

A little bit of a reminder that she wasn't doing this alone. "So…go upstairs. Find an empty bed and curl up in it. I'll handle everything down here, and if it's something the boys need specifically from you, it'll wait. I'll wake you in three hours, in time for lunch."

"That...that sounds like the most wonderful thing I have ever heard."

"I understand. Even if you have to bring her out here every day and nap each afternoon, we'll make it work. And Phoebe, eventually...you will get to sleep through the night again. I promise."

She'd just keep the fact that it might take seven years for that to happen to herself. There were some things a newer mother just didn't need to hear.

Sixteen

When Phoenix stepped into his father's kitchen around three that afternoon, he found his two youngest brothers and three tiny blond girls settled around the table, a plate of brownies in front of them, and a board game waiting.

Patton had a tolerant look on his face that Phoenix recognized.

Patton was far nicer than Phoenix had been at his age.

No surprise; all of his brothers and sisters were nicer than Phoenix ever was.

Well, all except Perci. Perci could be mean when she was angry as a kid. And Pan…Pan wasn't much better.

The housekeeper was there, at the stove. She turned to him when he walked in, a wary look in her pretty green eyes.

Phoenix studied her for a moment.

Phoenix had to admit she had a good body, and the blond hair and green eyes were attractive.

She was a very pretty woman. That had just sunk in. For an older woman, anyway. She had to be around forty or so, he thought. He wasn't very good at figuring out women's ages.

He could understand why his dad seemed caught up in her.

If it was just a physical kind of thing. His dad had been widowed, that didn't mean he was dead.

Not that it was anything serious or anything—his father had been head-over-heels for Phoenix's mother.

He didn't see his dad getting involved with a much younger woman with three kids to raise. The youngest one was still practically a baby. That was just crazy.

His dad was past that point in his life, Phoenix thought. Probably looking forward to the day Parker was out of the house and on his own, too.

So his dad could finally have a life of his own. He'd been twenty-two when Phoebe was born. His father had had no choice but to take over the ranch from Phoenix's grandfather. Not if he'd wanted to feed his family, anyway.

His dad had told him once that he'd vowed as a kid not to be like his own father, who had drunk too much and spent too much and who had barely squeaked by, with a bunch of kids who went to bed hungry too many times.

Phoenix's father had wanted responsibility more than anything. To *be* responsible, and have people see him as a good man. A family man.

His father had worked hard all of Phoenix's life to get the ranch to pay off more than it had.

He'd almost succeeded too. Until the wreck that had changed everything.

Something else they could blame Phoenix for.

He had a lot to make up for. Phoenix wasn't sure he ever could. Because he hadn't been paying attention, had thought he was superman or something, he had lost his mom and nearly killed his sister.

He'd only looked away from the road for an instant. Then Sadie Rutherford's car was right there.

Hard for him to forget that. The sounds, the smells, the sights. Perci's screams. His own tears. Even if everyone else had. Even if it had been Sadie Rutherford who had crossed that yellow line and not him. He had told people that, and they hadn't believed him. Until…he had started to doubt it himself. But Joel had found stuff to prove it. Everyone knew now.

It didn't matter.

Phoenix should have seen her sooner. Then there wouldn't be a stranger at his dad's kitchen stove, being paid to help his dad take care of Phoenix's family.

It was hard not to feel resentment of that.

"Hello, welcome back," the housekeeper said. "You're just in time for brownies."

"I'm good." But manners had him thanking her. His mother would have smacked him if he was rude to a woman being nice to him. "My dad around?"

"He's out in the barn," Patton said. "Him and Pete. Pip is on her way over for some reason. She's waiting for Miss Rhea to get there to watch the kids."

"Phoebe's sleeping. She's really tired," Parker said, a brownie shoved half in his mouth. "Glenna and us, we're watching Aria while Phoebe sleeps. Phoebe was up all night."

Phoenix looked at Glenna. "She ok?"

"The baby was teething, and your sister needs a rest. Are you staying for dinner? There will be plenty. Meatball subs, macaroni and cheese, and Parker gets to pick the vegetable."

The last thing Phoenix wanted to do was eat dinner watching *her* sitting in his mother's place at the table. It had been hard enough all those nights when it had been Phoebe sitting there.

But to have a stranger there? Yeah, no. He bit back what he wanted to say.

She knew, though. Her green eyes watched him like he was a snake ready to strike.

Phoenix looked at the brothers he had actually missed while he was in L.A. He wanted to spend time with his family. He wasn't about to let the housekeeper run him off. "Yeah, I'd like that."

"Great." He suspected she would have said more, but a baby cried from somewhere. She wiped her hands on a dish towel and turned toward the living room.

"Aria's awake. You'd better get her," Parker said. "Before she wakes Phoebe up."

"Yes, sir." Glenna ruffled Parker's hair as she walked out of the kitchen and smiled at Parker. She had a sweet smile. If it was genuine.

Yes, Phoenix could see why his dad had just agreed to bring her to Masterson with him. All she'd probably had to do was smile at his dad just like that. Give his dad some sob story about being down on her luck, and his dad would have been total putty.

Parker waited until she was out of the kitchen before looking at Phoenix.

"You'd better not scare Glenna away or be mean to her. Pete and Patton and me—we like her and voted to keep her. Forever." His little brother glared at him like he didn't trust Phoenix one bit.

Forever? Hell, she was *good*. "Why would I scare her away?"

"Just don't be mean to Glenna, or you'll make all of us mad at you again. Especially Dad." Parker just looked at him. The kid was seriously weird sometimes, but Phoenix would admit it. He'd missed his brothers and sisters.

He'd missed his father most of all.

Seventeen

PHOENIX WAS IN THE KITCHEN HOLDING PHOEBE'S daughter when Phil made it in for lunch. There was a look in his boy's eyes. One Phil had seen before.

Something had upset him. Phoenix was probably his most passionate, mercurial child, definitely the most creative, and he took things to heart.

Combined with the anger he'd directed at himself since the loss of his mother, and Phoenix was becoming someone Phil didn't quite recognize.

Or like, for that matter.

He'd kept telling himself that everyone had their own journey to follow. Phoenix would get there. It just took time.

"Son, glad to see you." Phil checked the rest of the occupants of the kitchen and dining room.

Glenna was quiet, a look in her eyes that concerned him.

Nerves.

And fear.

Glenna was afraid of Phoenix, damn it. What had his son said or done to put that look back in her eyes?

The kids were busy playing a board game at the kitchen

table, and they all spoke to him for a few minutes. Elly, too small to really play but wanting to be a part of everything, lifted her arms for Phil to hold her, a smile just like her mother's on her sweet little face.

Phil had to oblige. It had been a while since Parker was small enough to want held like that. She smelled baby-powder-and-brownie fresh, reminding him of his own girls so many years ago.

It had gone by so quickly. Phil missed those days so much sometimes. He hugged her again before putting her back in her chair.

"So where's Phoebe?" he asked after looking around a moment. He saw no sign of his oldest child anywhere.

Except the baby, anyway.

"She had a rough night last night. Aria is teething," Glenna said softly. "Phoebe's napping upstairs. We'll need to wake her soon, so she can eat lunch. She didn't eat much breakfast either."

Phil nodded, worry hitting him hard. This wasn't like Phoebe at all. "I'll get her down here."

"Great. I just made vegetable soup for lunch. And a loaf of bread. Parker and Patton handled the salad."

"I can't wait. Salad looks great, boys." There were chunks of vegetables that needed cut a bit better, but his boys looked proud of what they'd done.

Phil didn't miss the leery look Glenna shot at Phoenix.

He hoped his son hadn't done anything to upset her. Phil felt protective of her.

No denying that.

Phil brushed a hand over her shoulder as he passed. Just to comfort as much as he could. What he really wanted to do was pull her close and make her a promise—nothing was going to hurt her or scare her again. Not on Phil's watch.

Eighteen

PHOENIX'S DAD DID THINK GLENNA WAS A HOT woman.

Maybe that was what the woman wanted.

She obviously needed help with something, and she had three kids to take care of. Maybe she was thinking his dad had more money than he did. His dad had a house big enough for lots of people, money enough to pay the bills, and plenty of food to go around. Maybe she was looking for Phoenix's dad to take care of her and her kids.

It was possible she was a gold digger. His dad had started making decent money with his new breeding program. It showed in some of the changes his dad had made to the house.

It still smelled like *home*, though.

The kids put the board game away, the two older girls squabbling. The housekeeper handled it quickly, then took the baby from Phoenix.

She seemed competent at the job. Her girls weren't total brats. Parker and Pete seemed to like her ok. Even Patton, as shy as he was, seemed ok with her.

But Phoenix didn't trust her one bit.

Maybe his dad was just horny or something. He was still a guy—and Phoenix's mom had been gone for five years. Phoenix couldn't imagine going without sex for *five* years. Even if he was older, like his dad.

This housekeeper was right there in his dad's house, was very pretty, had a good body, and if she was flirting with his dad, of course, his dad would fall for it.

He looked at her again. No.

Even though she had to be around forty or so, she was an attractive woman.

Phoenix had met quite a few women in L.A. who were after whatever they could get from a guy and would use that to get his attention. It had happened to Phoenix when some girl had learned he was decent friends with Rowland Bowles.

She'd tried hitting on Phoenix to get in with Rowland. She had almost succeeded, too. Until Rowland had pulled him aside and caught him up on how women in L.A. worked.

He didn't think the housekeeper was from a big, big city like L.A. but Finley Creek wasn't exactly Masterson. Maybe she was looking at his dad like he was her meal ticket?

Her and those little girls of hers.

Phoenix was thinking about that when Phoebe came in, all sleepy-eyed and rumpled.

Still really pretty, though. His sisters were all really pretty and sweet. He was glad the guys they married appreciated them. They all deserved to be loved.

"You feeling better?" the housekeeper asked her softly as she handed over Phoebe's daughter.

"Honestly? I still feel nauseated. But thanks. I needed the nap badly."

The housekeeper nodded, then handed Phoebe a cup of tea she'd brewed. "This should help. Anytime you need a break, call me. Bring her out here, curl up, and sleep. Take advantage of all the help you can get."

"You don't have to do that."

"I want to. I don't know how many times I dropped my girls off on your aunt. I wouldn't have made it through their infancies without Robin and our friend Rory's help. Let me pay it forward."

Phoebe nodded. "I'm glad she had you."

"I am, too. And I helped with Robin's three whenever I could."

Phoenix had to give points for effort. She sounded genuine. But he'd seen good actresses a thousand times before.

Nineteen

It had been a long day. For all of them. Phil had looked at his eldest daughter and ordered her back to bed after she picked at her lunch.

That Phoebe hadn't protested told him all he needed to know.

Phil finished all the chores he could after lunch, and hurried back in, to give Glenna a hand with the kids. Just in case.

She was used to three. Not his two youngest, her three, and baby Aria on top. He stepped inside the back door, ready to walk into chaos.

Instead, Aria was cuddled against Glenna's chest like she'd been there a thousand times, tied against Glenna by a bolt of fabric, of all things. Sound asleep, her tiny fist in her mouth.

He smiled.

Becky used to use a strange sort of carrier with the kids, that left their little feet dangling. He'd always thought she looked ridiculous but cute.

Glenna had Elly and Emmy curled up next to her and Evey and Parker sprawled on the rug at her feet as Glenna read from a book.

The house smelled like tomato sauce and baking bread. Everything was neat and put in its place. The kids were calm and quiet and looked content.

She had handled the day just fine.

Glenna looked up at him with a sweet smile.

It was nice to come inside to be greeted by her smile. She was a very pretty woman, his new housekeeper. A very pretty woman, indeed. "Hi. Phoebe's still sleeping. Her husband called looking for her earlier. He's going to stop by and get her and the baby in time for dinner. I figured we could feed them so they don't have to worry about it."

"Phoebe have a fever or anything?"

Glenna shook her head. She handed the book to Patton, who had sprawled in the armchair nearby. Patton started reading where she left off. The younger kids sprawled out a bit more. A few more minutes and some of them would be asleep, too.

The woman worked miracles apparently.

Glenna stood and followed Phil into the kitchen. "Not that she's said. I think she's just exhausted." She looked down at the baby sleeping against her chest. "They have a real way of doing that."

"That they do."

"When Evey was this age, I had ridiculously high expectations for what motherhood *should* be like and what I was doing wrong in not achieving it. What I as a good mother needed to look like. It took me a few years to settle down into what it was. That, and Robin *thunking* me over the head and making me give myself a break. She yelled at me and told me I was being stupid—in the middle of the grocery store. A month later, I learned I was pregnant with Emmaline." She gave a rueful laugh. "I just about collapsed, bawling my head off, sure I couldn't do it. By the time I was pregnant with Eleanor, I was so numb I don't really remember a thing. Except...diapers, lots and lots of diapers."

Phil laughed softly. Her smile was soft with memories. And a bit sad. "Did you have help, honey?"

She shook her head. "Lincoln was never really involved with the girls. Other than the making of them, anyway. He didn't even ask for visitation during the divorce. He was just never that interested. He tried at first with Evey, but like everything else he ever did, he lost interest. Looking back, I think he just didn't know how to be a father. He had no staying power for anything, other than the military. But I figured that out, too. He needed someone to tell him what to do—it was why he liked the army. He never learned. Unfortunately, that meant us, too."

"I'm sorry."

"It's my fault. He was good at putting on a front. We had only dated six weeks before he asked me to marry him. Then he deployed two months later. Had three long deployments in five years. He'd volunteered, I learned. He liked the adventure and having the military being in control so he didn't have to make decisions himself. He came home, we got pregnant, then he was in a nasty accident. He was very reckless behind the wheel. Everything went downhill after that. And now I am here, with the girls."

Once again, he suspected her words hid a world of hurt.

Of secrets.

"And I am glad you are here right now." He cupped her cheek. Phil leaned forward and kissed her right on her forehead. Just to comfort. "I'm damned glad you found your way to me now."

Soft green eyes looked right up at him. Startled and a bit afraid.

He was still staring back when the door opened and two tall men walked in. Phoenix looked at him, suspicion on his face. "Dad? What's going on now?"

Glenna jerked away, so quickly the baby fussed. She soothed Aria and stepped over to the slow cooker. "D-dinner will be ready in about fifteen minutes."

Phil bit back a curse. There had been a rude tone in Phoenix's words.

One Phil definitely didn't appreciate.

He looked at his oldest son. There was a look in Phoenix's eyes that told Phil all he needed to know.

Phoenix was angry again—and his target was Glenna this time.

Glenna hadn't done a damned thing to Phoenix. His son wasn't going to make her feel uncomfortable or unwanted. That wasn't going to happen.

Phoenix was going to behave himself, or he could just take himself off again until he got a better attitude.

Twenty

PHOEBE STARED AT HER BROTHER LIKE HE WAS A total idiot. In that moment, that was exactly what he was. He'd come upstairs to supposedly wake her, now that Joel was there to get her.

She knew the truth; Phoenix had wanted to talk. To complain.

About Glenna. About his suspicions.

Phoebe couldn't help it. Even though she knew it would make him angry, she laughed. How could she not? She'd had the same thought just a few days ago.

"She's not after dad. At least…not in a bad way."

"How do you know? What do you really know about her?"

"Joel checked her references, and Dad's business partner and his wife have known her since she was pregnant with her youngest. Not to mention Aunt Robin—"

"Who we really know nothing about, either. How do we know this woman is even Robin? How do we know they aren't a pair of scam artists or something? Where's the proof she isn't out to seduce Dad and drain him dry?"

"First, there are far wealthier targets out there that don't require her moving all the way to Wyoming with three young children to find. Second, she's a nice woman who needed a job and a place to stay while getting licensed in Wyoming for her career. She's spent the last three years as a crisis counselor, Phoenix. Not exactly some evil seducer of men. Dad really likes her. And I emailed Charlotte as well. She had nothing but good to say about Glenna. Maggie also knew her slightly when she was in Texas. Glenna makes Dad smile again. In that way he used to with Mom. It's nice to see. He can be so shy with women."

Phoenix's expression darkened. Phoebe got it then. That was the real problem. Another woman was in their mother's place. Her brother wasn't ready to face the idea that there might be room for another woman in their father's life. Phoenix was struggling with change, too.

Weren't they all?

Phoebe hugged her little brother, though at six two and broad shouldered now—he'd filled out in the last few years—he wasn't so little.

"Look, Phoenix, Dad...is lonely. He needs someone, too." Maybe she wouldn't have understood it before Joel, but now she did. "That loneliness, it eats at you."

"So the first woman to come along, he just moves her in without thinking of the consequences? I think we've all learned our lessons there."

Oh, Phoenix. Her younger brother was so angry. With the world. With himself. She'd hoped that since he'd found his passion in life working in film that he'd also found some peace. Apparently not. "Is it Glenna you have a problem with, or any woman in Dad's life at all? I don't want him to spend the rest of his life without someone who loves him. He deserves that. More than any man I know, he deserves someone to love him."

Phoenix shrugged. "But why someone from out of town? You don't really know her at all."

"I know what I see. I see a woman who loves her daughters, who is a bit shy and insecure, and a woman who gets a look in her eyes when our father looks at her. One that says *she* can't believe she's that special. I think her ex did a number on her, and she's hurting, too. And maybe...maybe Dad will be good for her, too. And not just as a bank account with legs. Don't do anything to mess this up for him."

"Like I always do?"

"That's not what I meant, and you know it. Everyone knows you weren't at fault with Mom, Phoenix. We always have. We just didn't know how to fix anything back then." Phoebe had talked to a counselor herself since everything had happened. She was finding her own peace. Her sisters had as well. They were finding their own way. Moving forward. She just wished Phoenix would soon. "I know you don't like the changes going on. But our lives didn't stop when you left. They can't. Not mine, or the twins and Pan, or the boys. And definitely not Dad's. Give Glenna a chance. I did. And I am starting to see where she is just as good for Dad as he is for her."

As her brother stormed out, Phoebe pressed one hand to her rolling stomach and just watched him. Worried.

She meant it, she realized. She'd watched Glenna and her dad during lunch, too. They were good for each other, and Phoebe did like her. Quite a bit. Glenna was exactly who she appeared to be. Kind and empathetic, sweet and humorous.

Shy and wounded, too.

Phoebe thought Glenna was exactly what her father needed.

She wasn't going to let Phoenix screw that up for them. It was time she called a sister meeting. They had some planning to do.

But first...the soup she'd eaten for lunch was taunting her. Again.

Twenty-One

TWO DAYS AFTER HE'D FOUND HER CUDDLING HIS granddaughter in the living room, Phil went searching for her again. For a bit more personal care.

He'd gotten stupid, distracted by thoughts of her and the well-worn jeans she'd had on at breakfast. And sliced right through his arm with a box-cutter he was using to cut through wire in his workshop.

He needed her to help bandage him up.

But Glenna was a bit more squeamish then he had expected. He distracted her by asking about her life in Finley Creek. About what she'd been doing when she'd first met Robin.

Glenna had worked for social services, until she'd gone back to school to get her degree in counseling.

"So why did you quit?" he asked softly as her hands tended the cut on his arm. He could see specks of blue in her green eyes. Someone had to be close to her to see those. He liked that he was. He just stayed right where he was, breathing in the scent of beautiful woman.

"It's a hard job. And it took me away from the kids too

much. I had a supervisor who wasn't great. And who wanted to spend time with her own family—at the expense of others on staff. She was calling me in so often, the girls were spending more time with Robin and Rory than they were me—after my friends were coming home from working their jobs, too. It all blew up, and I ended up on probation. Ended up with even worse hours after that. So a friend told me about W4HAV. I applied, and they hired me. Even before I went on maternity leave six months later. I hadn't known I was pregnant at the time. Fortunately, Mel Barratt—the woman in charge of financing at W4HAV—insisted the insurance cover me anyway."

"I've met her. That doesn't surprise me. So why did you truly accept my offer?"

A sad, frightened look passed over her face. Phil cupped her cheek gently. He wanted to be gentle with this woman. And he loved touching her when he could. "The truth, honey. I'm not going to judge you. Sometimes, we all need a way out of something. What really happened to make you come to me? I know more happened than you told Phoebe the other day."

"My late husband's family are not what you would call good people. They would demand money from me—which I never gave them—harass me whenever they could. They started showing up at the kids' games and activities and making horrific scenes. It was awful—both embarrassing and frightening. A colleague at W4HAV—her uncle had to chase them off of the premises one night. He is a friend of Rory's from the Texas State Police. The girls started getting scared of every man who even resembled them a little. They hadn't ever interacted with Lincoln's family—he forbade it. But about a year after he died, they started showing up demanding money from life insurance policies they say he had. He didn't have any that I ever found. I even had Rory make some calls. If there had been something,

Rory would have found it. They don't have a clue where I am; I intend to keep it that way. That day his mother tried to take Elly from the preschool class at co-op, everything blew up. I tried to press charges, but I was told they probably wouldn't stick that well. That was the last straw. I won't have my girls afraid. And I won't have those people taking my children to do God only knows what with. She was high at the time. Her son was driving the car. And he wasn't much more sober. It terrified me."

Phil understood that on an intrinsic level. The way only another parent could. He had lived it the days two of his own girls had been taken. They had been adults. Had they been helpless children…

"You're safe here, with me. You and the girls. And if anyone ever shows up here, I'll handle it. I promise. No one will hurt you ever again."

She just looked at him, all big eyed and beautiful. "You are a kind man, Phil. I…hope you know that. I think the world needs kindness now."

"It does. It always has." To hell with it. Phil needed to do it. He lowered his head and brushed her lips with his.

She didn't pull away. Her fingers spread over his chest, and she gave a little hum. A beautiful sound.

He pulled back to make certain he had her permission to continue. "Can I kiss you again? I want nothing more in this world right now than to kiss you."

Words he never thought he'd say to another woman again, but words that felt so very right. He understood this woman. So much of what he valued himself was in her. Saw the kindness and love that she carried in her, too. How was a man supposed to resist that?

Even though every reason why he shouldn't be thinking those thoughts ran through his head.

Phil just didn't care. Nor did he care that she was just four years older than his oldest son-in-law. Or that between them they had eleven children who all made demands on their time in some way. Two of her children were younger than one of his granddaughters.

All that mattered was it felt right when he held her. And Phil wanted to keep on holding her forever.

MC

This was hunger and attraction and things she hadn't felt in a long, long time.

Glenna dropped what was in her hand to the small table, and then placed her palms over his chest again.

She wanted him to kiss her again.

Glenna nodded her head slowly. He lowered his head again. She leaned up on her toes.

Then she was wrapped up in his arms once again.

She could feel his heart, so sure and steady, beneath her hands. He tasted like the hot chocolate her girls had given him to make him feel better after his injury. He'd stopped in the door to the kitchen to talk to the girls, and they'd given him hot chocolate.

Which he'd accepted and thanked them for even though it was powdery and lumpy and a little cold. Made them feel appreciated and valued. He'd done it so easily.

This man was a wonderful father.

Was it so wrong that she found that attractive, too?

She kissed him, more actively participating now than she had before.

Just to answer questions she had of her own.

When someone yelled his name from the laundry room, Phil pulled away. Glenna just stared at him for the longest moment.

What was she supposed to do about him now?

She didn't have a clue.

Twenty-Two

AFTER THE KISS THAT NEVER SHOULD HAVE happened, Glenna didn't know what to do with herself. Thankfully, the kids kept both her and Phil busy until it was the kids' bedtimes. Then she and Phil retreated to their separate rooms.

And it was exactly what it was—retreating. She'd hidden herself away and called Rory for pointers on what to do next. Cautioning her friend not to tell Robin yet.

Robin would come riding up there, kids in tow, to give Glenna a step-by-step playbook of what should happen.

She rather had control issues, that woman. Much like a few of her nieces, actually.

Rory had just laughed and snickered the entire time. Said she'd told Glenna so—and to keep an eye out for a brother of Phil's for her when she came visiting.

Glenna and Phil didn't have a moment alone for the next day and a half.

Everything was far too chaotic for that. They had a party to go to, apparently.

Glenna and the girls had been specifically invited.

Phil bundled her and the kids up into his van, and took

them through the country several miles—to his brother's semi-retirement-slash-birthday party.

She hadn't even realized what she was agreeing to at first. Until Parker and Patton were excitedly making plans for her and the girls to go with them. Parker had even made a list of dishes they were going to take.

She suspected Parker wanted to show her off a bit to his cousins.

Meeting new people wasn't exactly easy for Glenna, but the boys were so excited that she'd nodded yes before she'd really thought through what it meant for her and the girls.

She was taking them into a group of strangers. That was never easy for her.

She wanted to make *connections,* she reminded herself. This was a good place to start.

It felt like a date.

Glenna tried to tell herself that it wasn't, but the words wouldn't come.

It felt like a date.

She could do this.

It couldn't be a date—not with her three daughters and three of his own sons, plus one grandchild, riding with them. In a passenger van. It was an old van, but it practically purred. It was the only vehicle big enough on the property for her, Phil, and all six of their kids, plus Ivy, who had somehow shown up with Phil while her father handled an emergency at the hospital and her mother was off helping her mother-in-law somewhere.

Ivy had had a great time playing with Glenna's girls. Glenna had gotten several hugs herself as the hours had passed.

It had been a beautiful day. Phil had done a few chores outside. Then he'd been with his boys and granddaughter all afternoon. And her girls.

He included her children as easily as he did his own. He didn't single them out as "guests," nor did he push them aside in favor of his own family. And when an argument had broken out between Parker and Evey, he had handled it fairly.

The man had the patience of a saint. That was for sure.

And the rear end of a Roman god.

Her cheeks flamed as that thought snuck in again. She'd lusted over her boss again—Glenna really needed to stop doing that.

It was going to get her into some serious trouble one day.

She'd come into the living room to find him bent over, fresh from the shower, picking up the pieces to a board game that had gotten spilled everywhere. He hadn't had his shirt on, and his jeans had been riding low.

There wasn't an ounce of fat on that man anywhere she had been able to see.

He was nine years older than her, but he really didn't look it. Except for the gray.

Her fingers had almost tingled with the urge to touch. To see if those muscles were as toned and sleek as they looked.

They grew them—and aged them—well in Wyoming.

Who knew a man picking up toys was so sexy?

She was going crazy. The fresh mountain air had driven her completely mad. There was no other answer for it.

Either that, or it had triggered her latent hormones.

Maybe that was why there were so many Tylers in the county? The mountain air made them all horny, and they just spent their time reproducing like rabbits?

She looked over her shoulder at the seven children behind her. Him, her—a van filled with seven children.

She never would have imagined this even a month ago.

It was no wonder she was feeling so confused.

Twenty-Three

SHE LOOKED GORGEOUS. PHIL HAD ALMOST swallowed his tongue. The jeans were obviously newer, and the mint-green sweater probably hand-knit. It clung to her soft curves in all the right places. Glenna had enough curves for a man's hands to hold the way they were meant to.

He had to admit it: his hands did burn to do just that.

Phil was going to have to keep himself in check. He couldn't go around lusting after his housekeeper.

It was obvious she was gun-shy where men were concerned.

That had been behind part of his invitation today. He'd wanted her to see that not all men were threats. He suspected that was a lesson this woman needed to learn.

She had that look in her eyes that said someone somewhere had hurt her before. A soul-wrenching, bone-deep kind of hurt, that only time and love could truly come close to healing.

He'd seen it before. In his daughter Pip's eyes, after that bastard Jay Gunderson had attacked her when she'd been all of nineteen.

He hated seeing it in Glenna's eyes now.

He was going to do his damnedest to make certain that look never ended up in her daughters' eyes.

Not on his watch.

"How far of a drive is it?" she asked quietly. Nervously. She wouldn't admit it, but the snow—and driving in it—bothered her quite a bit. It would take time for her to get used to it. In the meantime, he'd just drive her wherever she needed to go.

Phil rather liked taking care of Glenna when he could.

"A few more miles. There're only about three miles between Michael's place and mine. We are using a private service road here. It's listed as East Tyler Road on the maps. The boys keep the roads clear using our tractors and such. We'll just go slow, and we'll be just fine." He reached out and patted her hand, then checked the rearview. All seven kids were fine, though two were gearing up to go at it. "Girls, no fighting in the car, ok?"

"I'm sorry." She immediately turned. He squeezed her hand again, stopping her.

"It's ok. Brings back memories. The twins were always pestering Pandora. Then Phoebe would get involved. She always had to protect the underdog. Then they'd gang up on the boys. I kind of miss the chaos of having them all home. The girls have only been married around two and a half years. Some less than that."

"But Ivy…"

"Ivy's adopted, honey. She came to us when she was two. Her parents have been married the shortest amount of time. A little over two years." Phil kept his voice down, conscious of the little ears behind them. He did a quick check in the mirror —they were under control, with Pete keeping them in check.

He really was a good kid, his second son. Phil was damned proud of all his kids.

"I didn't know that."

"She came into the emergency department when Perci was working one night. Ivy ended up going home with Nate as his foster daughter. Perci went with her—the two of them basically never left. Ivy's ours now. The adoption was final a year and a half ago."

"That's wonderful. That she was able to find a family that quickly."

Phil nodded. "It was meant to be. Ivy's a Tyler now. Well, Masterson, but we'll ignore that part."

She laughed. He loved to make her laugh. It sounded so sweet. And always seemed to surprise her a little. "You like all your sons-in-law."

"I do. I can't think of four men better suited to my girls. I want my girls happy and loved. And I got that now."

Twenty-Four

PHIL TYLER'S BROTHER NICK WAS A BONA FIDE FLIRT, and a total ladies' man. Glenna really liked him—and she knew better than to take him seriously. Even if she suspected the appreciation in his eyes was *real* when he looked at her.

It had been a long time since she'd been looked at that way by an attractive man—and now here there were two. Focused right on her. Glenna didn't know what to think about that.

Robin had warned her to watch out for Nick Tyler. She could see why.

But...he really didn't hold a candle to his older brother.

He was a few inches taller than Phil—Phil admitted he was the runt of the litter—and about three years younger.

He also seemed to like Glenna quite a lot. It surprised her at first, until she realized the truth. Nick was flirting with her—to get under his older brother's skin.

Nick was most certainly needling Phil on purpose.

Phil was sticking close to her side, hovering. Overprotective.

At least, that was what she thought at first. Until it sank in —he wasn't being overprotective—Phil was being possessive.

She'd never had a man be possessive over *her* in her entire life. Lincoln hadn't, and neither had the two men she'd been involved with before she'd met Lincoln. She hadn't dated much —she'd never really had time for it, having worked to support herself since she was a teenager in high school. She'd wanted her college degree and hadn't been able to qualify for much student aid.

Glenna knew the truth, too. Dating had always been something she'd struggled to figure out. Even in her forties, it wasn't something she knew how to do.

She settled at a table near the back of the large barn that had been converted into a family meeting hall and type of event center and watched the crowd around her. They were all related. That was taking a moment to sink in.

Elly shifted in her arms, fussing a bit as she fell asleep. Her youngest still needed a nap occasionally, and running around with a pack of at least three dozen kids had overstimulated and exhausted her. Glenna rocked, while watching the people around her.

Watching Phil.

He had a presence about him that made others seek him out. Calm, leadership qualities. A way of talking that was open, honest, and respectful. Intelligent.

Kids seemed to like him, too. Going to him for hugs and hellos and attention. Her girls especially seemed to seek him out. They adored him. She knew a lot of it had to do with his personality, but a part of her wondered if it had to do with her girls not having had a father in their lives for so long. Not that Lincoln had interacted with them often—he'd only held Elly maybe four times in the three months she'd been alive before his own death. She had never understood his apathy where his daughters were concerned.

Parker ran up to her side, concern on his face. "Is Elly ok?"

He peeked at Elly's face, pulling the blanket someone had given

Glenna to cover her up with away gently. "Are her ears hurting her again? We can tell Perci and Nate. They can check her when she wakes up and make sure she's ok. Nate's a good doctor. The best."

He was so earnest in his concern that it warmed her heart. Glenna held out her arm to him. He was at that age where hugs were uncool, but he hugged her immediately. She kept it quick. He had cousins around—he couldn't look like a dork, he'd told her before. And...his heroes Rowland Bowles, the famous movie producer, and Hunter Louis Clark, the Hollywood actor, were *right there* in the hall with Phoenix and their cousin Nikki.

Parker was totally trying to act supercool tonight. His ultimate dream, she suspected, was for Rowland Bowles to ask him to be in another movie someday.

"She's ok, I think. Just tired. Are you having fun?"

"Yes. It's cool being one of the older kids for once."

"I bet it is. When your Aunt Robin gets here, you'll get to meet Philip and Wesley. They are a year younger than you." And looked quite a bit like him, but with Robin's darker auburn hair.

"Great. We can do lots of stuff. I have some things already planned." He patted Elly's back again and adjusted the blanket over her, then took off. Breezing through like a storm. Glenna smiled as she watched him. He really was a good kid. So sweet at heart. And very much like his father.

Patton found his way to her eventually, too. He wasn't the kind of kid who liked large crowds. Glenna had figured him out pretty quickly. He settled at the table—between her and the wall. She shifted a bit to act as more of a barrier for him from the rest of the room. Patton tended to get overstimulated by noise, too. "You doing ok?"

"Just loud." He had a plate of cookies and potato chips and a soda. "I figured I'd take a break and get a snack. Is Elly feeling any better yet? I saw her crying earlier."

Phil joined them in time to hear the question. "Everything ok?"

"She's fussy tonight. I think she may be a bit overstimulated. And a little sniffly. She's prone to colds and things." Glenna shifted the blanket around her two-year-old. Her baby. She hadn't exactly been thrilled to be pregnant at almost thirty-nine. At that point, she had known her marriage to Lincoln was all but over. But she had never regretted Elly for even a single moment.

She loved her daughters so much. She saw an identical love in Phil's eyes when he ruffled his son's hair and stole a cookie from Patton's plate. When he put his own body between his quietest son's and the rest of the room to give Patton the oasis he needed.

Yes.

Great fathers were highly attractive.

Even more so than their playboy younger brothers.

Pete stopped by. He had two cans of soda in his hands that he placed in front of Glenna and his father. "Here. You two look like you need a break."

He spoke with them a moment, then took off after some of his older cousins. To speak about some ranching technique he was passionate about and already researching. He'd stopped by to ask Phil his opinion. Because he valued it.

"He's more into the land than I ever was," Phil said. "I'm thinking about giving him twenty acres up by the cabin this spring. Let him try some of his experiments and techniques. That land was my grandfather's. Peter was named after him. I figure it's fitting it goes to him. I just need to get the rest of the kids together to discuss it. Make sure it's ok with them."

"That's a wonderful gift." And perfectly suited to his son. "You, sir, are probably the best father I have ever seen. I mean that. Your kids are lucky to have a father like you."

He cupped her cheek lightly. "And your girls are damned blessed to have you, honey. Damned blessed."

"I hope so." Glenna smiled at him. An answering heat settled in her stomach when she recognized the expression in his blue eyes. Phil Tyler liked what he saw when he looked at *her*. "But...I really need to visit the ladies room right now. Elly's been kneeing me in the bladder for an hour. I'm about at my limit."

"Hand her over, honey. I've got you covered." Just like that, he reached for her baby.

Glenna handed Elly over without a second thought.

Because she trusted him on the most intrinsic level of all.

She trusted him with her daughters.

Twenty-Five

THEY WERE TREATING HER LIKE SHE WAS A QUEEN. All of them.

Phoenix listened to Rowland flirting with his cousin Nikki with only half his attention. The rest of his focus was on *her*.

Queen Glenna.

Maybe he was being jerk, but...it was like his father hadn't even realized he—or his sisters, who had all four shown up with their kids and their husbands and even their mother-in-law and her new husband—existed.

No. His dad had a new batch of kids now.

Phoenix watched as Parker hugged her, as Patton sat down right next to her, and Pete brought her a damned soda. And his dad—touching her like that? In front of everybody. When she'd even been flirting with his uncle Nick right there—in front of his dad.

Had she been trying to make his dad jealous or something?

"That was absolutely beautiful," Nikki said, nudging Phoenix's shoulder from where she sat. She had been sitting most of the night, and Hunter was treating *her* like a queen for some reason. Pampering her and watching every move she made.

Phoenix was almost convinced the man actually had a thing for Nikki or something. Which was just crazy. Nikki was gorgeous—although a bit bossy, and had always been—but Hunter wasn't the kind of guy to get involved with a woman if he couldn't be serious.

He had told Phoenix that himself. When he had been answering some of Phoenix's questions about being an actor. Phoenix loved working for Rowland and *making things* like the movies and series he'd been involved in already. But Rowland kept hinting he wanted Phoenix on the big screen.

Phoenix wasn't certain he wanted that for his future.

Hunter and Rowland were good guys. Hunter wouldn't put the moves on Nikki and then just leave. Phoenix was almost certain of it.

"What was?"

"Your dad and his new girlfriend," Nikki said as she wrapped up Phoenix's nephew Griffen in a blanket Pan had just handed her. "How they looked at each other."

He almost made a stupid remark about her not seeing what she thought she was. But Nikki...didn't see all that well in actuality, and he wasn't going to be a jerk just because he didn't like what she had to say.

Even though she made jokes about her eyes, he suspected she was still pretty sensitive about it.

Nikki was likely to smack him—or have one of her brothers do it. They could be total assholes when they were mad sometimes. The Tyler temper that was so legendary in Masterson—it was real.

Phoenix had inherited it himself.

Sometimes he didn't think his father had, though. Nothing seemed to faze his dad sometimes. Especially lately.

"She's not his girlfriend. She's his housekeeper."

"Yeah, like that's going to stop a man," Nikki said wryly as their cousin Maggie joined them with her own baby in her arms. Nikki looked at Maggie. "Phoenix doesn't seem to think Uncle Phil's new *housekeeper* can also be his girlfriend. I mean, it's not like that happens at all in Masterson or anything."

Maggie gave a wicked laugh. Maggie plopped her almost one-year-old son into Phoenix's arms. "Sure it does. Here's the living—and sleeping—proof that it does, right next to Pan's proof. So what's going on with Uncle Phil? Is it serious?"

"No." He almost bit it out, then remembered the sleeping baby in his arms. He'd always liked kids. They didn't look at you like you were a total screw up or anything. "She's just his temporary housekeeper or something. Until her licensing or something comes through from Texas."

"What does she do?" Nikki asked.

"She was one of the counselors at W4HAV," Maggie said quietly. "I had a few group sessions with her. Grief counseling, mostly. W4HAV really helped me while I was down there. I worked through some things about Mom and Dad's...death. And what happened after with the social worker. Glenna is really good at listening. I think she's great for Uncle Phil actually."

Phoenix fought down the anger at what this cousin had gone through, too.

"Glenna has a great reputation down there. She was one of the favorite counselors. And I met her girls several times. Sweet kids." Maggie looked right at Phoenix. "She's a nice lady, and if your dad is involved with her, that is absolutely wonderful."

"Yeah. Wonderful."

Everyone seemed to like her and be in favor of it—except for him.

Phoenix was so damned tired of being the odd man out in his own family.

Chapter 25

Glenna was washing the kids' sheets when someone knocked on the front door of Phil's house. The kids—including Ivy—were in the basement, watching a Harry Potter movie while Elly napped again. Elly was fussing quite a bit today and had fallen asleep in the living room—along with Phil's youngest granddaughter Poppy, who Glenna had agreed to watch for the afternoon. Glenna closed the dryer door quickly and headed to the door herself.

A woman Glenna had met at the party the night before stood there.

She had brown hair and a ready smile and was about Glenna's size. She was also around twenty years older than Glenna. "Hello, Glenna. I hope you don't mind me just stopping by. I'm a few minutes ahead of Nate and Perci, and wanted to speak with you, if you have time."

"Of...course." She had no idea why Phil's daughters' mother-in-law would want to speak with her. "Would you like something to drink?"

"Water would be fine." She stared at Glenna, obviously taking her measure. Glenna didn't stare right back, but she wasn't going to be cowed. "I have heard good things about you. I figured to stop by and check you out for myself."

Well, she was taking care of this woman's grandchildren at times. There was that. "Oh?"

She would have asked more, but a baby cried from the living room. "If you'll excuse me..."

Rhea followed her into the living room, where Elly was curled up on a blanket in the floor, and Poppy was fussing in the playpen nearby. Rhea scooped her granddaughter up quickly. "Hi, sweetheart."

Elly was waking, too. Glenna shifted course a bit and scooped her own daughter up. She felt warm. Too warm.

Warmer than she should. She placed one hand on her daughter's forehead to check, as Rhea quickly changed Poppy's diaper.

"She's probably hungry," Glenna said. "She's been asleep for a few hours."

"We'll get her taken care of. I didn't know the girls were out here today."

"Ivy's downstairs with Emmy and the rest of the kids. Pete's watching them."

"Good. That gives us time to talk." Rhea looked at Elly. "She not feeling well?"

"She's a bit fussier than normal for the past few days. I'm probably going to find a pediatrician soon. She's prone to ear infections, that kind of thing." Her baby was clinging tightly. Instead of following her sisters around like their shadow. That told Glenna something was definitely wrong. Her arms tightened around Elly.

"Nate carries a bag in his truck. He might have an otoscope. We can give her a good look. I am retired, but I still miss working with the little ones sometimes." Rhea placed Poppy in the high chair. Glenna had the baby's lunch already prepared. She warmed it up quickly.

Then turned to the woman watching her. "What can I help you with today, Dr. Masterson?"

"I heard you are a licensed mental health counselor."

"In the state of Texas. I am getting ready to start the process here in Wyoming." She had made the decision to stay an hour after Phil had driven her and the kids home the night before.

It had felt *right,* being here. As if Masterson was where she was meant to belong. As if she was finally *home.*

"Good. By the time that is finished, I'll be ready. You can come work for me."

"Excuse me?"

"I'm creating my own little version of W4HAV here in Masterson. It's needed. And I need someone to help me run it part-time. Rumor has it you might be just the woman I need." Rhea shot her a significant look. "Unless you are planning to be Phil's housekeeper forever?"

Twenty-Six

SHE WAS PREOCCUPIED. PHIL COULD TELL THAT BY the time he'd been in the house fifteen minutes. She was busy peeling potatoes for potato soup when he'd finished his shower and rejoined her. He grabbed a knife and sat down at the table next to her.

The way he once had his Becky. Echoes of his past with her would catch him unawares at times. Would sting.

He would always love that woman. And miss her with every breath. But there was a living, breathing woman in front of him with something on her mind right now.

"Care to talk it out?" he asked quietly after he'd peeled a few potatoes. "What's on your mind?"

She looked up at him. Surprise was on her face. "Rhea Masterson is in basement with the kids."

"I saw her car."

"She's offered me a part-time position. Fifteen to twenty hours a week."

"Rhea is a good friend. I've talked to her some about what she's wanting to do here in town. Gave her some ideas from what I know about W4HAV."

Glenna nodded her head. "This charity she talked about did have a lot in common with W4HAV."

"Twenty hours isn't much."

"I want to do it. I need to know I'm helping people." Serious green eyes just watched him. As if she was almost afraid of what he'd say. "I'm just trying to figure out how to make it work, and figure out childcare for the girls."

"We'll figure it out together. Working for me is flexible, honey. I promise that. As for childcare—if I'm here, I'll keep the girls for you. Or Pete might be willing. They'll be safe here, I promise. You don't have to worry about your girls while you're out there helping. Not for a minute."

She just stared at him, like she couldn't believe what he was saying. "They've never stayed with a man before. Not even their father, Phil."

"Then it's time they started. Unless you want them growing up thinking children are just women's work? We Tylers don't believe that for a minute." He was only half teasing, but he had his suspicions when her eyes got even wider and her mouth trembled. Damn, she was so sweet he wanted to gobble her up. "I'm just teasing. But I mean what I said—the girls are going to be fine here. I want you and the girls to feel like this is your home, too."

He shocked her—it was obvious on her face—when he covered her small hand with his own much larger, much rougher, hand.

"You don't have to be afraid here, Glenna. I will never let anything hurt you again."

Twenty-Seven

HER SISTER PERCI AND PERCI'S DAUGHTERS WERE there when Phoebe pulled in a few minutes before dinner was usually ready. Joel had gotten called in to deal with something a few blocks from the diner and Phoebe didn't want to be alone tonight.

Her mother-in-law was there, too. For once, she didn't have her six-foot-five, rather-impressive, brand-new husband trailing after her like a besotted puppy. Phoebe laughed to herself when she remembered how put out Joel had been when his mother had told him she was remarrying so soon after Gerald had returned to Masterson County permanently.

Joel was still getting used to the idea of his mother being married to his father's best friend now. Of actually *sleeping* with a man at all.

Phoebe thought it was sweet.

They were both widowed. They were both powerful, dynamic personalities. And they had been lonely. Anyone with eyes could see that.

Now Gerald was enjoying being *grandpa* to Daniel Masterson's grandchildren. He'd said once in front of Phoebe that he wanted to be there for his late best friend's family, just as he knew Daniel would have been there for his if the roles were reversed.

He'd meant it, too.

Phoebe liked the romance of it, too.

And together? The two of them were as forceful as a F5 tornado in what they wanted to accomplish.

Phoebe strongly suspected her own daughter was going to be just as stubborn and full-speed-ahead as Rhea Masterson.

Glenna and her father were at the table, talking quietly together, when Phoebe pushed open the back door.

Phoebe paused for a moment and just looked at them.

They looked very sweet together.

Rather like Rhea and Gerald, actually.

Her father had that look in his eyes again. She'd seen it at the party, too.

One that said he knew where he belonged. And it was right next to Glenna.

And Glenna—there was something so sweet and almost poignant about how she looked at Phoebe's father.

Her father stood, took Aria from her, and then the diaper bag. "Hi, sweetheart. Glad you are here."

He always said that to all of them. Because he meant it.

"Hi. Joel got called in again. I didn't really want to be alone tonight," Phoebe said around a yawn.

"Still tired?" Glenna asked.

"Yes. I'll eventually sleep again, sometime, right?"

Glenna patted her on the shoulder. "Eventually. Just remind yourself of how much trouble you get to cause her when she's a teenager. Vengeance. Or so I've been told. Wait until she's seven and knows *everything*. That's fun, too."

Yes. But Phoebe had watched Glenna in action. The woman had it totally together, and managed all three of her girls so well. Phoebe didn't know if *she'd* ever get to that point.

Rhea came in and was already reaching for the baby. Phoebe's father laughed and handed her over. He still had half a bowl of potatoes in front of him to peel. "Hi, sweetie. You look like you need a nap."

"I do. We're still teething." And it made Aria so fussy Phoebe wanted to cry right along with her. Phoebe felt like crying a lot lately.

"Dinner is a bit later tonight than planned," Glenna said. "Why don't you go rest for a few minutes?"

Phoebe didn't want to, but the idea of even twenty minutes…was so hard to resist.

"I think that's an excellent idea," Rhea said, sending Glenna a significant look. "Your little one is waking, Glenna."

"Thanks. She's starting to run a temperature, too."

Phoebe tried to keep up with the conversation around her, but Aria wanted her mother and Phoebe was busy rocking her. Sometimes Phoebe missed things, even with the hearing aid.

"Well, Nate is pulling in. I'll grab his bag and have a look," Rhea said.

"Thank you. I haven't even thought about finding a regular pediatrician yet."

"Dr. Shane Lowell. The man is totally amazing, and the piercing blue eyes and tiny hiney don't hurt either," Rhea said. "I'll get you his number. But as for tonight, I think Nate and I can handle things just fine."

Phoebe watched as her family just kept doing what they had always done.

Taking care of each other. And anyone else who needed it. They were making room for Glenna and her family, too.

As Glenna's middle daughter came in with a question, Phoebe's father leaned down to her as naturally as if he'd done it a thousand times. He ruffled her little blond pigtails and helped her before sending her back out of the room with

Phoebe's niece Ivy. They were best friends now and told everyone who saw them that.

Her dad looked ten years younger tonight. He looked... happy. Like he felt needed again.

Maybe having the kids around was good for him, too.

As the back door opened again and Phoenix came in steps ahead of Perci's husband, Phoebe made her dad a silent promise.

If Glenna made him happy, Phoebe was going to do everything she could to help them figure that out together.

Twenty-Eight

GLENNA HADN'T KNOWN WHAT TO THINK WHEN A call came the next morning just as she was getting ready to make her first solo drive into Masterson County to pick up the antibiotics Nate had prescribed for Elly. He'd had some antibiotic samples in his bag that had gotten them through the night and would last through to the next morning, but he'd called in the remainder of the prescription for her at the local pharmacy.

But the phone call changed her plans a bit.

Had her at the diner, meeting a dark-haired young woman with big green eyes and a shy smile.

This woman was Phil's nephew's wife—and she had been sent by Rhea. To capture Glenna.

Or so it felt.

Jude Tyler had asked Glenna to meet her for lunch during her errands.

To talk about the job offer Rhea had made.

They were coming at her from all sides, it seemed.

Glenna wanted the job. She just wanted it to work out for the girls—and Phil and his boys—as well. Without her feeling like she was taking advantage of him or wasn't holding up her end of the bargain for him, too.

The diner was a nice place. It was her first time eating there, and it immediately brought back memories of Mamaw's Place in Finley Creek.

They apparently had the same decorator back in the eighties or something. It almost didn't look like it had been updated since. Glenna loved it immediately. It reminded her of home.

She'd waited tables at Mamaw's Place for four months between Evey's birth and Emmy's to help make ends meet, after all.

The woman she was there to meet led her to a back table, shyly thanking her for coming.

They hadn't been seated two minutes before the waitress arrived—with a bowl of fruit and yogurt that she placed in front of Jude.

"Compliments of the hot, extremely sexy guy in the back booth," the seriously stunning waitress said, laughing. "I'll get your drinks in just a moment."

"Thanks, Marin."

Glenna gawked at the other woman. "Some random guy just ordered you dessert?"

Jude nodded, a wry expression in her eyes as she picked at a strawberry. "He's not random. He's actually very sweet. And he's trying to make up for...the morning sickness."

"I'm sorry?"

"That's my husband back there. Michael. He's Phil's nephew number two. I know they are hard to keep straight. I am fifteen weeks pregnant and having trouble with morning sickness. I didn't eat breakfast. Michael was worried—and now he's trying to tempt me. Fruit is about all I can keep down this early in the day. I'm sorry he interrupted."

"No, I think that's beautiful. It's wonderful that he's so concerned."

"It's not something I'm used to," Jude said. "My first husband was very violent. And I was young. Michael is the exact opposite—with me."

That wasn't exactly something Glenna had expected her to open with. "You don't have to bring up painful memories."

"I called your previous employer in Finley Creek. She had glowing references for you, but she did say you had some trouble that was following you. Your husband's family?"

"Yes. But they don't have the money to come this far."

Jude nodded quietly. Glenna suspected she was a quiet woman overall. "This is a support group position, funded by private donations, organized by the sheriff's mother. It's not very high paid—yet. I know you have children to support. It's at most going to be part-time. Is that going to work for you?"

Glenna appreciated how to the point the woman was. She found herself relaxing with Jude quickly. "Yes. I think it will. Phil has volunteered to watch the girls sometimes. His daughters, too."

"They are a wonderful family. I was Ivy's case worker and got to know them then. Michael...came later. They're very close. All of the Tylers here are close." Jude smiled softly as she looked toward the rear of the diner. "It takes some getting used to. But...they are a beautiful family."

"Yes. They definitely are." She'd left the girls with Phil. He'd had breakfast ready, had the kitchen clean, and told her to take the day off, take some time for herself today, if she wanted. He and the boys would handle everything and would call if Elly needed anything he couldn't manage. She was going to take a few hours, run errands for her and the girls, grab Elly's medicine, and then learn her way around the town. Before heading back to her girls. And the boys.

And Phil.

The man...she'd dreamed about him last night. Dreams that

still made her cheeks burn when she thought about them. That hadn't happened to her in years.

It took her a moment to tune back into what the younger woman was saying. "The program isn't off the ground yet. And it will take us all working together to make it happen. But if you are willing to put in the elbow grease, it's yours."

"I would like that. Very much."

"Wonderful. I wish I could offer you a position with my office, full-time, but we just don't have the funding yet."

"You know, I think I would rather help counsel. I did that for W4HAV. And it felt like I was making a real difference. I would like to feel that again."

"Instead of riding the hamster wheel that is social services? I totally understand, and welcome aboard. If you have any questions for me, my number is on this card. And Rhea's is on the back. We can do this. It'll help the people of Masterson County."

Glenna nodded as hope filled her. It was nice to feel like she had a purpose again. Like she could help people—without having to watch over her shoulder to do it.

Their lunch arrived. Glenna's eyes widened, seeing how much food it was.

Jude laughed at her comment. "I know. When I was single and living a few blocks away from here, I'd order two of the specials on Monday, and they'd pack it in to-go containers for me. I swear I'd eat off them for a week. Now…leftovers don't last the night. Michael burns a lot of calories working the ranch. I wish I had half his energy. If he doesn't finish off the leftovers, three of his four brothers live with us for now. We go through a lot of food there."

Glenna got her chance to see this husband in action a few minutes later. To her surprise, five tall men, who looked very much like Phil, filed by their table. Men she'd met at the party. But there was no way she could figure out who was which yet.

The first two said hello to Glenna and kissed Jude on the top of her head. Two, identical down to their tennis shoes, kissed both of Jude's cheeks. Making her laugh quietly and blush.

The fifth man did much more, giving her a kiss that Glenna could just see the passion humming through.

When he looked back at Glenna, Glenna understood the appeal.

The man was gorgeous—and he did look very much like his uncle. He was several inches taller than Phil, and about fifteen years or so younger. But the resemblance was there. He greeted Glenna politely, then asked how his wife was feeling. Promised to pick her up at five.

His hand lingered on his wife's stomach. He toyed with her long, dark hair.

He touched her like he loved her. Valued her.

Then he stepped over to another table as a redheaded woman settled down on a bench with a little blond toddler. A toddler Glenna remembered trailing after Emmy and Evey at the party, too. Phil's great-niece, she thought.

The toddler ran straight toward the five tall men, laughing.

Jude's husband scooped her up as another brother hugged the redhead.

Jude smiled at Glenna. "There's Maggie. She spoke highly of you, from her time at W4HAV. She's going to help with W4HAV when she's not busy with Blessed Reunions."

"Oh, she works for Mel still?" The familiar names eased some of her tension. She never had done well by surprises. This place...it really was a different kind of world in Masterson County. Where you could let your toddler run free in the middle of a diner full of people and know she was perfectly safe. Where you could see your family when you walked through town.

Where people knew you by name.

That was something she and the girls had never really had.

Glenna ached for that for her girls. So very much.

Finley Creek was a bit too big for that. With Lincoln's para-noia keeping them trapped at home all of the time, they hadn't had the chance to build those kinds of ties. And since his death, she had just been so busy getting the girls through, and dealing with Lincoln's family, paying down debt, and *building* any kind of a life.

It was different here.

She wanted that. Wanted it for her girls so badly she almost ached.

Glenna thought about that as she drove back to Phil's. Toward home.

She was starting to feel like maybe this was where *she* was supposed to belong now, too.

Masterson had been the right decision for all of them, after all.

Some of the burden and worry she'd been carrying since making that decision lifted. And Glenna started to feel like she was able to breathe freely again.

She was smiling as she slipped in the back door, carrying the bags of sweatshirts and jeans she'd picked up for the girls— and a few for Parker she'd found that were too good to pass up, and were his favorite movie themed—at the thrift store she'd found six blocks from the bookstore. She'd put them upstairs in her room, sort them, and take off the tags before washing them. The girls needed more warm clothes now that they were going to stay in Masterson permanently.

Her, too. She'd have to go back to the thrift store, see what she could find. Or dip into her savings and order them all a few more things online. Rory had rented out her house for one hundred and twenty dollars more than Glenna had anticipated. The first check would be coming soon.

Things were settling nicely. She was...happy. That had her smiling again as she rounded the landing.

And smacked straight into a hard male chest.

Promptly forgetting even her own name.

She looked up—into the dark blue eyes that had teased her in her dreams the night before. "*Phil*. I didn't see you there!"

Twenty-Nine

THE FIRST THING SHE NOTICED WAS THAT THE CHEST
was completely naked. The second thing she noticed was that
the chest beneath her hands was hard as a rock. Lean. Well-
toned.

Then she saw the scar.

"You've had heart surgery?" she asked before she thought
about how nosy the question was.

He nodded, covered her fingers with his own, keeping her
hands trapped against all that male skin. "Found an issue about
four years ago. Genetic, correctible. Shouldn't cause a problem
now. I did lose two brothers to it before we realized what it
was. It's relatively rare, apparently. Thankfully, it didn't pass on
after us. Except for Patton. He'll need minor surgery in a year
or two—his won't be as invasive as mine, as mine was emergency, but we're all good now."

"I'm sorry about your brothers. How many were there of
you?" The flesh beneath her palms was warm. She wanted to
keep touching him.

"There were eight of us. Now it's just Ned, Nick, Bill, and
me. Our youngest brother, Bruce, took off years ago with a

much younger woman. Left three young daughters behind. We're not sure where he's at now or if he's even alive. Haven't heard from him since. His girls are in their early twenties now; their mother took off the year before he did."

"I'm sorry. That must have been hard for his kids."

"It was." His hands had slipped down. Wrapped around her waist. "Honey, you keep pressing up against me like that...I am just a man."

Glenna's heart flew into her throat in an instant. Her eyes met his.

There was hunger there. Real hunger.

Not just the expression that would be on Lincoln's face when he decided he wanted sex and she would do for the night.

She had a feeling Phil was actually seeing *her*. And not just any random warm body to play with.

She would never be one hundred percent certain who all Lincoln had slept with in the last few years of their marriage. He'd told her when she was pregnant with Elly that he didn't find her hot any longer. Didn't want to bother having sex with her if all she was going to do was be pregnant after.

That was when she'd first suspected he was having an affair.

She'd asked him. He hadn't denied it.

Not exactly something a woman with two young children, morning sickness and stretch marks had wanted to hear at the time. She'd told him the truth—if that was the case, he could just keep his hands to himself.

He had. Mostly. There had been once or twice when he hadn't. When he had been insistent that he still loved her, and it would be good for both of them if they were *intimate* again.

She had given in. Because she'd wanted to preserve their marriage. Glenna should have left him long before.

But if she had, she wouldn't have Elly. She had no real regrets.

Phil's hands felt nothing like Lincoln's. The expression in his eyes was definitely not like her ex's.

It was just her and Phil and heat between them.

Glenna's tongue darted out to moisten her suddenly dry lips. "Phil..."

"Don't be afraid. I will never hurt you..." His head lowered. Then she was being *kissed*. Like she'd seen his nephew kiss Jude today. A real kiss. One with heat and...caring.

Wow.

Glenna's hands clenched on his strong arms. And she pressed closer.

Glenna kissed him back.

MC

HE PROBABLY SHOULDN'T BE KISSING her. But Phil didn't care. He'd wanted to. The sweatshirt and jeans she wore weren't exactly the sexiest of outfits, but they made her look real. Alive.

He wanted his hands on the flesh under that sweatshirt.

Wanted it real bad.

But Phil hadn't been at this stage with a woman in almost thirty years. He wasn't exactly certain what he should do next.

So he just felt. There wasn't much else he could do.

He slipped one hand beneath the sweatshirt and spread his fingers over the soft skin of her back. Glenna had silky soft, perfectly smooth skin.

He wanted to touch her all over. Wanted her to let him do that. Wanted her to let him hold her, too.

Phil wasn't ready to push, though. Not yet.

Glenna was the kind of woman who required more coaxing, for one thing. More finesse.

Hell, Phil was just a rancher. There was no real *finesse* in him anywhere. Open and honest, real feelings. That was what made a Tyler man.

That was what he could give her. If she'd let him.

She was kissing him back. That was what mattered now. Phil just held her right there on his upstairs landing.

He stayed right where he was, holding her, until the sound of a small herd of buffalo hit the bottom of the stairs and kids calling out "Mommy!" and "Dad!" had them pulling apart like they'd just been engaged in the most dramatic secret yet.

"The kids have found us. Run!"

Glenna's green eyes widened, and she laughed. Still wrapped up in his arms.

Right where he wanted her to belong.

Thirty

THE KIDS KEPT HER DISTRACTED ENOUGH OVER THE next few days that she didn't have even a minute to think about the kiss. Either of the kisses. Or the man attached at the other end.

Phil...was good at confusing her. That was for sure.

The weather had cleared a bit, and the roads were passable, and Elly's ear infection was healing quickly.

The kids were going stir-crazy stuck inside the way they were. Phoebe and Glenna were going to have to come up with a battle plan—before the kids killed each other and turned on Phoebe and Glenna next.

That meant...homeschool field trip time.

They were going to hit the local library, then their cousins' bookstores and thrift stores for discussions on being business-people, and then the diner in town for lunch.

Followed by a tour of the Talley Inn—the part of the building that was rumored to be haunted. Parker was especially excited about going ghost-hunting that afternoon. He was talking about eventually filming a ghost-hunter movie there. As soon as he wrote the script—and talked his cousin Nikki's friend into letting him film there.

Someone was going to give them an inside look at how the inn worked in general from a business perspective, and how the legend came into be, in particular. Family history of the owners and everything.

That was a part of Pete's research project on how legends were formed and societal and social factors that contributed to such myths, for an advanced-placement class he was taking online through a local satellite college.

Phoebe had arranged it with a friend of her cousin Nikki.

Glenna was looking forward to it. Phil's third daughter had the day off, and she showed up to go with them, her two daughters—Ivy and Poppy—in tow.

Ivy was five months older than Emmy. The two had already proclaimed that they were best friends forever. They were utterly adorable—two sweet little blond girls who walked around holding hands and chattering in little girl voices to each other.

Evey was perturbed by the very possibility of Emmy having a best friend and her not. Elly couldn't care less. She was too busy following Parker around, again.

Parker Tyler was Elly's *hero*. Everyone could see that.

Patton and Pete and Parker were remarkably tolerant of it all.

They were waiting on lunch at the diner—complete with half of the Tylers inside, to her surprise—when her phone rang.

She grabbed it quickly. It was a new phone number. Only Phil and a few other people had that number.

"Where are you right now?" Robin's familiar voice came through the line. Glenna smiled. It had been almost a week since she'd heard from Robin. Which was entirely unlike her best friends—they checked in with her every day, usually.

Glenna had been starting to get worried.

She'd gotten one text back from Rory in three days. That was...weird. She was half afraid something had happened.

"The Masterson Diner. Why?"

"Great. Stay there. I have a surprise for you."

"What?" She shifted the phone to one side and Elly to her other hip. Her youngest liked to take the phone and talk every chance she could get. Even to bill collectors. "What's going on?"

"Just stay put. You'll know when you can move again. Seriously. Freeze, woman."

Her friends always had been a little weird. Glenna looked at the just arriving food, at the kids whooping at the arrival. They were some seriously hungry kids, apparently. Perci had promised them ice cream for dessert. "Our food just arrived. We're not going anywhere. This...is a lot of food. And they've been promised ice cream."

"Good. Five minutes. I'll be calling you back in about five minutes." Robin laughed wickedly after she spoke. She always had been a brat.

"Robbie, what is this about?"

"You forgot what day it is again, didn't you? Seriously, Glenna Marie? This is the third year in a row. I told Rory you would."

It took her a minute, but Glenna got it. "I did. I forgot again, didn't I?"

"Of course. Five minutes. I'll call you back in five."

Glenna disconnected, then looked at Robin's nieces, who were watching her curiously from faces that looked a great deal like Robin's. "Your aunt. She is up to something. Probably for my birthday. They make a big deal out of it every year."

"Today?" Perci asked. Her young daughter nursed discreetly, while her older daughter was busy eyeing the still steaming French fries on her plate. Ivy had been cautioned to wait a minute before grabbing and stuffing her face.

"Yes. I usually don't do anything special. Except with Robin and our friend Rory. I was so busy, I forgot what today was." Busy thinking about Phil. And what that kiss had meant between them.

What she wanted it to mean, too.

Forty-two.

It had crept up on her so fast. She'd been thirty-five when Evey had been born, almost thirty-seven with Emmy, and thirty-nine with her Elly.

"It comes fast, ladies. Especially when you are busy being mommy. I wouldn't have traded a minute of it for anything."

"Me either," they both echoed. They laughed. They were beautiful young women. She liked Phil's four daughters very much. She could see so much of Robin in all of them.

It made her a bit more sentimental than usual.

Her phone rang. "Yes, what are you up to?"

"Turn around." Rory this time.

Just as Evey shouted and pointed behind Glenna's shoulder.

Glenna turned. She squealed, almost as loudly as her daughter had.

There *they* were.

Her two closest friends in the world. Three beautiful children stood in front of them, looking around curiously.

The twins had a poster with *Happy Birthday, Aunt Glenna!* written on it in their hands. Little Becky, two months older than Elly, held a balloon tightly in one fist.

Tears hit her eyes. She jumped to her feet. "You're here! You're right here! Oh my goodness! I can't believe this. I'm going to cry. How did you manage this?"

"It took some doing, but here we are. And we're staying for a while, too," Rory said. A look passed between them that Glenna didn't miss. But that was for later.

Right now... "You're here."

She put Elly in her chair next to Ivy.

Then she was being hugged by her two closest friends in the world. And things felt a lot better than they had before.

Thirty-One

ROBIN AND RORY HAD RENTED A HOTEL ROOM. THE room connected to one they'd rented for the kids. They settled all the kids in for a marathon movie session while they settled in the other room—for a marathon talking session.

Robin and Rory must have hugged her fifty times each.

She had missed them so much. They were so entangled in each other's lives that they'd see each other almost every single day. And had for years.

To suddenly not have that had hurt. Video chats, texts, and phone calls hadn't been the same.

She'd been reluctant to stay at the hotel after the tour, but Phil's daughters had assured her that their father would have insisted anyway—and that the two of them would see to it that their father and brothers could take care of themselves for one night. Perci had pointed out that they had better be able to, or she'd kick their butts.

Glenna had introduced Perci and Phoebe to their aunt again.

It had been a little awkward, at first.

It was bittersweet. Robin had lost her relationship with her family because of the actions of one evil man. Glenna would never understand how that had happened. Would always hurt for Robin and Perci and the others that man had so callously hurt.

They had kept in minimal contact through the years, but not what it could have been.

Glenna blamed Robin's husband for that. They had married when she was twenty-four, and he had been extremely controlling. He had despised her relationship with Rory especially. He'd tolerated Glenna. Glenna and Rory had convinced her to divorce Doug ten years ago. Then she'd gotten pregnant. Robin had stayed with him another six years for the kids' sake. There was more that Glenna suspected Robin had never shared.

She'd probably still be with him if he hadn't had an aneurysm and passed away while sitting at his desk while at work one day. She had been pregnant with Becky.

Rory had a happier story, to some extent. She'd married at twenty-nine, to a cop she'd met on the job before she'd transferred into forensics. They had gotten along well enough. Until she figured out that he wasn't emotionally "married" at all. Not after the loss of his first wife, who had been lost in childbirth. Along with their third child.

Rory had helped him with the older two boys when they'd been married. They were still close.

He just liked having someone at home waiting for him, and a very attractive woman in his bed every night for fun and games to help him take his mind off the job. He hadn't been interested in anything *more* emotional than that.

Rory had filed for divorce that next week. They'd remained friends somehow.

Glenna suspected Keaton Price was still attracted to Rory a great deal.

The woman was gorgeous, after all. Gorgeous, sassy, passionate, intelligent, tough, and hilarious. Rory just didn't see what *she* had to offer to a man, though. Keaton had done a number on her confidence.

They all had their issues. That was for sure. But they had each other.

She never wanted to lose that.

"What are you thinking about so heavily?" Robin asked after the younger girls were tucked in and Robin's twins were watching another movie.

"Us. The past."

"Go on," Robin said, grabbing little girl shoes and shoving them into Becky's little girl suitcase. She held up one lone sock. "Becky's or one of yours?"

Glenna just shrugged. "I have no clue."

"We'll count feet in the morning."

"This wasn't exactly how we pictured things," Glenna said, laughing quietly.

"No, I can't say that it was," Robin said, arms full of boys' tennis shoes now. "We made mistakes along the way. Did a few things right, too. But life...has a way of not turning out how we hoped. Better in some ways, not so great in others."

"Phil's daughters...they are all so wildly in love with their husbands," Glenna said. "It's beautiful to see. And it has me thinking—about my own choices. I just am not certain I ever felt that way for Lincoln."

"You loved him," Rory, always loyal and protective, said.

"I did. At first. Until things just felt like they fell apart." Lincoln had pulled away from her within months of Evey's birth. He hadn't wanted to be a father. He hadn't wanted to be a husband. Eventually, he just hadn't wanted Glenna either. "If he hadn't been away so much, I'm not sure we would have lasted as long as we did."

"Sometimes, you just...status quo things," Rory said. "I know it's tougher when you added the kids, too. It has to be."

Rory had experienced a stillbirth when she was in her early

thirties, at not quite nine months. There had been complications that required a tubal ligation at the time to prevent further pregnancies.

Glenna knew how that had hurt her friend, though Rory said she was ok with it. That it was a good thing she and Keaton hadn't had a child, after all. That Keaton *was* a child in far too many ways for her to think about, especially with two teenagers at home at the time.

She was happy being aunt to Glenna and Robin's kids. She took on that role with enthusiasm, spoiling the kids every chance she got.

"When I married, I had all sorts of dreams. Now...I'm not sure what my dreams are supposed to be. I'm forty-two. When did that happen?"

"No kidding. I've not been in Masterson in twenty years. I've been away longer than I lived here," Robin said. They climbed onto the king-size bed, three plastic cups and a two-liter of soda plus ridiculously child-friendly snacks in front of them.

They kept their voices to a whisper, mindful of the children sleeping just fifteen feet away, through the open door.

"My dreams are for the girls to grow up loved, and safe, and as full-speed ahead as they can be," Glenna said. "But...once that is done, then what? I'm not used to being rootless. To not having a real plan. I feel far more in control with a plan."

"You like it here, with Phil?" Robin asked, a worried tone in her voice. "It not working out?"

"It's working out really well. So well, I'm afraid of what will happen when it ends. The girls...they adore it here. Adore him. Love the boys, too. And all the babies around just thrill them. They fit in so well. I...it feels like that big TV-family kind of place. But we're not Tylers. And I don't want the girls to get hurt. To get settled in here and something happen, and we have to leave suddenly, destroying everything we've built."

"If you love it that much, make sure that doesn't happen," Rory said bluntly. "Robin's brother-in-law, he's a good boss?"

"Yes, but I'm not a housekeeper, Rory. I'm a licensed counselor. I'm used to helping people. I...have a part-time job offer. They are trying to build a counseling center here. Like W4HAV. I'm going to work fifteen to twenty hours there. Phil offered to watch the girls while I work."

"Why...that fiend!" Rory said, shooting her a look that said she thought Glenna was worrying a bit too much—again. Glenna was the worrier of their group—Robin and Rory, the *warriors*. "Do you trust him with the girls?"

"Yes. Absolutely. That's the problem."

"Because you've never really trusted anyone with the girls, except Rory and me."

Glenna nodded. "That's part of it. And...Phil..."

"What about him?" Robin asked.

"He unsettles me."

"In what way?" Rory asked, suspicion in her tone. She'd spent time as a patrol officer before switching to forensics. Suspicion was second nature to her. "Safety? I mean, let's be honest: Robin hasn't seen him in twenty years. She could have a skewed view. No offense, Rob."

"None taken. Glenna, spill."

"He, it's not that. It's..." Glenna's face flamed as she tried to put her thoughts together. She was forty-two years old. She shouldn't be embarrassed talking to her best friends. That was just...juvenile. "He is attracted. *Very* attracted, or so he said. He has kissed me. And I have kissed him right back. It's crazy. Just kissed him right there at the top of the stairs, with the kids running around below. The last thing I need is to be attracted to a man with eight kids and seven grandkids—and I strongly suspect an eighth is on the way. He has a granddaughter older than two of my children. And I'm living in his house, which makes it even more awkward. I'm dependent on him for the roof over my head, my children's head, the food we eat, he pays for. What if this goes wrong? Lincoln and I just sort of fell into a relationship. I was the comfortable old shoe from the very beginning. And there hasn't been anyone since. I've not have a real attraction to a man in more than thirteen years. I have no clue what it is I am supposed to be doing here. What steps to take next. Or even what I want."

Robin just gawked at her. "You've been making out with Phil on the landing. Well, this was not something I expected."

"Isn't it? I mean, I've seen the guy and *wow*, I'd be tempted to pull him into the barn for a roll in the hay," Rory—always the most outspoken person Glenna had ever known—said. Even if Rory had never rolled in the hay with anyone in her goody-two-shoes life. "And she's right there in his house in front of him. Tempting him, too. All Glenna-the-good-witch-ish, with sweetness and light and baking cookies and cuddling babies. As pretty and sweet and loving as she is, maybe this guy is just as confused as she is by her. It might take some investigating here. So—tell me—what did he say after he kissed you?"

"Nothing, really. Evey and Parker were arguing and...we haven't really been alone together since."

"How does he react when that happens? I know Doug would get really angry with the boys if they interrupted him when he was...intent. Would yell," Robin said quietly. She didn't speak of Doug often, but when she did, it made Glenna want to take a page out of Rory's book and threaten to kick his ghostly ass.

"Not Phil. He just...he's wonderful with the kids. But when he looked at me after...no man has ever really looked at me quite like that. Or...I haven't noticed anyway. And I do with him. So tell me: What am I supposed to do?"

"Well, you just keep going. See what happens. And know that whatever the fallout is, you'll make it through. Because you have us, too. And...Robin has some news we've been waiting to share."

Glenna looked at her redheaded best friend. "What?"

"I've been let go from the hospital. They had to downsize. I have a severance package. I'm going to use it to come home, at least for a few years. I really want to give the kids a chance to know their family. To build the kind of connections that I don't have."

"She's leaving me behind forever," Rory said bluntly. "But we think it's best for the kids."

"The boys didn't do as well in school this year as I hoped." Robin's boys had a few challenges, but were hard workers. Robin had struggled to get what they needed from the Boethe Street elementary school for two years now. It was the worst school in the city—one reason Glenna had chosen to homeschool. "I want to get them out of that school system."

"I'm going to be in charge of handling renting out her place as well. And I'll visit every chance I get," Rory said, hugging Robin one-armed quickly.

"You're moving to Masterson." Glenna stared at Robin. Saw the nerves in her friend's light blue eyes. Understood the fears at every level. "Soon?"

"Yes. One week. Before another month's bills are due. I'm going to talk to the school system here before I head back to Finley Creek. Determine whether the boys will finish out the year in public school here or if we'll homeschool the remaining two months or so. I...am actually up here to look for a place for us to live, too." Robin gave a scared little laugh that broke Glenna's heart. "And an actual way to support my three children. I have some savings and Doug's pension, thankfully. I can stay home with the boys for two months if I need to, to help the boys. But...I'll need more than that."

Glenna wrapped her hands around Robin's. She knew

exactly what the other woman was feeling. "I can talk to Phil. See if he knows of anyone hiring."

"I'll find something. Even if it's just dumping trash cans at the inn for as long as I have to. I did that when I was eighteen, before I left. Maybe…maybe I need a reset. I'm almost thirty-eight years old and starting all over again. That's me."

"Me, too." Glenna wrapped her arm around Robin. Rory echoed the movement from the other side. "We can do this, you know. We just need to convince Rory to move up here, too."

That wouldn't ever happen. Rory had been building her rental business for some time. She had elderly grandparents in Finley Creek that she would never leave, and her mother was in Barrattville, along with a sister twelve years younger.

Unlike Glenna and Robin, Rory had real roots to Finley Creek. Ties she wouldn't want to break.

"I'll be up as often as I possibly can. What else am I going to do with my comp time? Chase Charlotte and her buddies around to make sure the little brats don't get into trouble again? Half of major crimes already *does* that. The rest probably need to."

Glenna laughed. That was a distinct possibility. "Someone's got to do it."

"So…talking about Charlotte reminds me…," Robin said. "How do Phil's kids feel about him kissing the housekeeper in the kitchen?"

"I…don't think any of them saw. And it was the upstairs hallway." Glenna seriously hoped not. That would make things beyond awkward. "I haven't had a chance to get to know all of them well. Phoebe, mostly. And Pete, Patton, and Parker, of course. They are wonderful boys. They are so tolerant and patient with the girls. Although Parker and Evey bicker quite a bit. Probably because they are the most dominant personalities. Pete is so calm and responsible. Even at his age, you just get the feeling he'll be able to handle anything. And Patton, he's the quietest, sweetest kid. Parker...he's so mischievous. I caught him putting a rubber rat in the washing machine. He was trying to scare me. He just laughed when I caught him. He's already full of questions of when his cousins Philip and Wesley are going to get here to play with him. And the babies are so sweet. They are everywhere. Emmy and Ivy are great friends already. It's beautiful here. I'm glad I came here. No matter what happens with Phil, this is where I want the girls to be."

Robin laughed softly. "Sounds to me like this is exactly where I need the kids to be right now. But I'm terrified. I don't know if it's because of how I left or that I'm afraid it won't live up to my memories. Or just the fact that I've always been terrified of change."

Glenna did know. She knew exactly how Robin felt.

They spent hours just talking. Like they had so many nights before.

Thirty-Two

SHE LOOKED TIRED. BUT IT WAS A GOOD KIND OF tired, Phil thought, as his housekeeper came in the next morning—minus three little girls.

"Where are the girls?"

"They stayed at the hotel for the day. Plans are to explore the pool. Robin and Rory even grabbed them swimsuits from Finley Creek. They think of everything, those two. Part of my birthday present is some time to myself, apparently."

"Well, welcome home." It didn't feel awkward saying that at all. "And happy birthday, honey."

"So where are the boys?"

"They all headed home with Phoebe and Joel. Patton and Pete are helping Joel with some remodeling chores, along with the rest of Joel's brothers. Parker is supposed to help Phoebe with the baby. At least that's what he said when he was packing his backpack. He seems to be worried that Phoebe is not taking good care of herself lately. He's determined she's going to take it easy tonight."

"So…we're alone?" Green eyes had widened slightly.

Phil nodded.

That was exactly what they were. Completely alone.

No kids...anywhere. Just him...and the beautiful woman in front of him.

The idea of spending the entire day with her tickled his brain. He had a few things he had to get done outside today, but...the rest of the day he'd planned to clean out the remaining corner of the basement and get the shelves installed before the boardgames and books multiplied like rabbits and started trickling *up* the stairs next.

"When will the kids be back?" she asked softly. "What should I do about dinner?"

Phil shook his head. "They are staying overnight tonight, too. The girls?"

"Spending the night at the hotel again, too. Robin says she'll drive them out here tomorrow around noon."

He had her all to himself. For the next almost twenty-four hours. Phil gave a quick thanks to the man above.

Not that he expected anything to happen between them, but this was the first alone time they'd had—other than after the kids were all in bed and he and Glenna were both exhausted to their toes.

His day had gotten a hell of a lot brighter.

"I've got a few things to do outside. Then I'm going to work on finishing a few things downstairs. If you want, I could use your help." Spend time with her. Talk to her.

And if he was lucky, maybe kiss her at least one more time. Or convince her to just sit on the big couch down there next to him. He would like that, too.

"I'd be happy to help." She looked around at the spotless kitchen—Phil wasn't exactly a slouch when it came to household chores either—and all the laundry folded and ready for each kid to put their own away. Just her two younger girls would need her to help them. "I don't have much else to do

today, apparently. For a family of four, you all seem pretty suffi-
cient. I almost feel a bit unneeded."

"Oh, you're needed, Glenna Carnes. Very, very much so."
The heat hit her cheeks instantly. Phil laughed. Yes. He was
going to enjoy the day with this woman. Every single minute of
it. "I'll be back in about an hour, honey. We'll get started on the
basement, then."

"Great. I'm going to call Robin, check on the girls. Make
sure they haven't taken over the hotel and staged a coup or
anything. See how she's doing." A worried look passed over her
face. "She's moving to Masterson. Next week. At least for a few
years. She lost her job and is going to find a place to live up
here. If she can find a job."

"While I'm glad that girl's coming home, I hate that it's
under those circumstances. She should be able to ride in
triumphantly after what she went through. What kind of job
does she do?"

"Admin. Mostly. Receptionist and hospital billing for five
years or so now. She's extremely good at organizing an office
and a bunch of minions. Scarily so."

"Her sister was the same way. She could organize the world.
Let me make a call. I have a nephew with his own trucking
company, him and my brother Nick. They were talking about
needing someone to run their office. As for a house...Jude, she's
getting ready to rent her house out, too. Would probably give
her the family rate. But...that probably won't work, honestly.
It's Clive Gunderson's old place. The sheriff who ran her out of
town back then. Maybe I'll see what else Martin has available.
He has a good four or five houses he's working on getting ready.
If not, I'm sure there's something around. Someone in the
family will know. We'll find her a place before she needs it."

Glenna gawked at him. "You can just...make things happen?
Fix things?"

"I wish I could. But here in Masterson, Tylers take care of each other. Robin might not be a Tyler by blood, but it's close enough. Hell, she lived with me for three years. She's always going to be family."

"You, Phil Tyler, are a different kind of man than I am used to."

Phil couldn't help himself. She just looked so wide eyed and almost innocent. He wrapped his hands around her waist and pulled her closer. And kissed her. Right there in the kitchen.

This time, there were no kids ready to interrupt them at the slightest drop of a hat.

That thought hit him like a two-by-four once again.

There were no kids to interrupt *today*.

"Phil?"

"Kiss me back, honey. There are no kids around to interrupt us now," Phil said, lifting her lightly until she sat on the table. "Let me kiss you? There is nothing I want more right now."

Glenna nodded, almost shyly. She made him want to be gentle. Phil understood that.

Becky had been all fire and youth. Becky had wanted what Becky wanted. Phil had been content to give her what she wanted—especially himself. He had fallen hard for her in a matter of a month. Quick. And right.

It tended to happen that way for Tylers, sometimes.

Glenna was as different from Becky as a woman could be in so many ways, yet she was like her, too. For a moment, he asked himself if that was what it was. Here Glenna was in his wife's place. In his house. His life. With his kids. Even with Becky's sister.

Maybe a part of him wanted her in his arms, too, because it just made sense.

But as he looked into soft green eyes, he understood the truth.

He wasn't trying to replace Becky with Glenna. Not at all.

It was *Glenna* as she was that was fascinating to him. Drawing him.

Consuming him.

He had never expected to feel this way about a woman ever again. Not after burying Becky.

His hand skimmed up the back of Glenna's sweater. Until he could tangle his fingers in soft blond hair not yet touched by gray.

Nine years separated them. But that didn't seem like so much now. "Just kiss me back. We'll figure out where to go from there."

Glenna pressed closer to him. "I...am not really sure what to do any longer. It's been so long...and...I..."

"That's two of us, honey. Two of us. I was married for twenty-four years, and never even thought about another woman. This...is new territory for me, too. I've not even kissed a woman in five years. I never thought I'd feel this way again. Let's just feel it together."

That was exactly what they did.

Somehow they moved from the kitchen and back up the stairs, until he had her in his room, and they were completely wrapped up in each other.

Thirty-Three

She had slept with her boss.

She had slept with her best friend's brother-in-law.

She had slept with a man who had seven grandchildren.

She had slept with a man who wasn't the man she had married.

But when Glenna woke after they'd drifted off in each other's arms, she found she didn't have a single regret.

Not even one.

Now she understood what Rory had meant when she said sometimes it just felt like it was supposed to.

Phil was watching her, one hand running up her naked spine lazily. "You ok?"

"Yes. I think I am."

She'd made a choice when he had asked her if she wanted him to stop after the kisses in the kitchen had turned hotter than she ever imagined they could.

Somehow they'd ended up in the room he'd shared with his wife.

That had given her a bit of a pause. She would admit it. Until he had asked her what was wrong and if she wanted to stop.

He'd repainted the room, he'd said. Gotten a new bed a few years ago. Said he'd had to, to let her go. Said he had let her go.

She had understood that, too.

She and Lincoln had been divorced when he had died, but she had still grieved him. She'd grieved the idea of him after they'd split up as well.

Phil had distracted her after that, with a soft kiss and a promise that he would stop the instant she'd wanted him to.

She hadn't wanted him to.

Not even for a moment.

He was the only man she'd been with since her marriage had ended. She'd thought it would be far more awkward than what it was. Even the discussion about *birth control* hadn't been as awkward as it could have been.

But it hadn't. He'd felt...right.

Both safe and exciting at the same time.

But now...now it was time to face the music. She couldn't just heedlessly hop into an affair with her employer. She had never been that reckless in her life. "So what now?"

"Now...we talk. Figure out what it is we both want. And where to go from here. Because, honey, now that I have you in my bed, I don't want to let you go. But with six kids in the house, well, we have to take their needs into consideration, too. No matter how much I want to shout to the heavens that you want to be with me, just as much as I want to be with you. We have to make certain to keep the kids' needs first."

It was in that moment that Glenna knew the truth.

She'd just fallen for Philip Tyler completely. Hopelessly.

And she had no idea what she wanted to do about him now.

So she stayed right where she was, until the sounds of someone calling for him came from downstairs.

Downstairs. Where they'd left half their clothes.

Glenna's cheeks flamed at what it meant. What was about to happen. This was not what she had intended at all.

"Get changed in your room," Phil said. "I'll deal with him. And then...you and I can go to town. Have dinner somewhere nice. Just me and you."

She took her cue from him. "I think I would like that very much."

Her first date in years. She was glad it was going to be with *him*.

Thirty-Four

His dad's truck was right there, and the back door was unlocked. His father had taken to making certain the doors were locked when the house was empty after that bastard Gunderson had attacked the twins that day. The housekeeper's SUV—small and not very practical in Wyoming—was right there, too.

A bright blue reminder of everything that was getting under Phoenix's skin.

All of his cousins and his sisters were talking about how great Glenna was. The Great Glenna, the solution to all of Phoenix's dad's problems.

He'd watched her at the party, too. Saw how sweet she had looked.

Maybe he was wrong about her. Maybe she was exactly as she appeared to be. Just a single mother working hard to take care of her girls, who happened to catch the eye of the man employing her.

Pip had said it was so sweet to see. Pan thought it was hilarious, Perci had told him to keep his nose out of it and let it happen naturally between Glenna and his dad, and Phoebe had just smiled at him when he'd asked what she thought.

Then she'd told him Glenna was perfect for their father and Phoenix better not screw it up—or she'd hand him his head on a platter. With salt and pepper. All in the same annoyingly sweet Phoebe tone.

Even Nikki and Maggie and Junie and Em and Auggie thought she was the greatest thing to cross into the county in years.

He just didn't get it.

What was so special about her that his whole family thought she was so wonderful?

He called his dad's name again as he stepped into the kitchen. That's when he saw...

Lingerie. On his dad's kitchen table. His dad's jeans right there. Hell. It looked like something staged from a damned movie. He knew exactly what had most likely happened.

"I didn't realize you were coming by," his dad said from the back steps leading upstairs. He casually walked through the kitchen, grabbing the evidence of what he'd been doing with his damned housekeeper. Wearing just a pair of flannel pajama bottoms.

Phoenix's cheeks flamed when his dad picked up a lacy blue bra that had landed on the floor by the table. His dad carried the clothing and undergarments into the laundry room and tossed them into the washing machine. When he turned back to Phoenix, there was a questioning expression on his face. "Are you just here to visit?"

"That's ok, right? I didn't interrupt your—" Hell, what was he supposed to call it? Roll in the hay with the housekeeper? He wasn't stupid enough to say that out loud at all. "Good time with Glenna, the housekeeper?"

"You aren't interrupting anything," his dad said. But there

was a warning in his words. It just had Phoenix's back going up instead.

His dad had been having sex with the housekeeper—right in the middle of the day. When Phoenix's brothers could come in at any time.

Although... "Where are all the kids? You two send them away so you could...get down and dirty in the kitchen?"

Thirty-Five

PHIL LOOKED AT THIS SON OF HIS. WHY WAS IT always Phoenix? They had been struggling together since the night they'd lost Becky. Phil was tired. He just wanted to find peace again. But he wanted peace for his son more than anything. "You can't keep going on like this. Saying whatever you want. Making an ass out of yourself with the people who love you."

"I'm an adult. I can do what I want. Say what I want." Phoenix looked toward the stairs, when they heard the telltale squeak of the floorboards.

Glenna was up there. *That* was where Phil wanted to be. Not down here dealing with Phoenix.

"No doubt about that. But is this the kind of adult you want to be? Alienating everyone who loves you? Where will you be then? Walking the world alone? That isn't somewhere I think you would want to be."

"That why you messing around with that woman? You're lonely?" There was so much sarcasm and disdain in the boy's tone Phil bit back his temper.

Then he thought better of it.

Maybe they had soft-pedaled with Phoenix too much. It was time for some tough love. "Watch your tone when you talk about her. She's a nice woman who deserves respect. And your mother and I raised you to treat people with that respect. Or have you forgotten that?"

Surprise was in the eyes so like Phil's own. The boy had grown up tall and strong and smart. But the attitude…

He had thought Phoenix had lost the chip on his shoulder years ago, after everything that had gone down with his sisters. He was almost convinced Phoenix had moved on a bit.

Something had changed. Something major. "What's happened to you, Phoenix? Talk to me."

"What's happened? I come home and find you've replaced her. Just put another woman there like Mom didn't mean anything."

"Your mother meant almost everything to me, son. Everything. She was my world for twenty-four years. When I lost her, I thought the biggest part of me had died alongside of her. But I kept going because of you kids. Now…it still hurts to have lost her. It will every day. But I'm not dead, too. I can't live like I am. Today just proved that to me. You're just going to have to understand that. And I won't have you acting like a brat in my house."

"Afraid I'll embarrass you in front of your girlfriend? Are you sleeping with her in Mom's bed?"

For the first time in his life, Phil actually wanted to slap his son for the hateful words coming out of his mouth.

But he had made himself a vow when Becky was pregnant with Phoebe—he would never raise a hand to one of his children the way his father had him and his brothers. Never.

"Watch it. Or you can take yourself back to the inn for the night. What I choose to do with Glenna is between the two of us and has nothing to do with you. If you would just give her a chance, you might find you like her."

"Like everyone else does? They just moved her right in like she belongs here. No questions or hesitation. Just, hey, here's this woman, let's just let her move in and take right over."

"Yes. I pay her to do that. To help with the kids so your sisters can build their own lives. Their own futures. Isn't that why you took off to Hollywood? So you could have your own life as well? What is so different about that? I can't do it alone. The house and the boys—or *life*, Phoenix. I deserve to be happy. To be with someone that I can be happy with. I could have that with Glenna, if I don't do anything stupid to mess up." He kept his words low. Between him and his son.

Voices carried in this house. The last thing he wanted to do was have Glenna hurt by what Phoenix and he might say.

He wanted to protect that woman from any hurt in the world at all.

"You? I didn't think you messed up anything. Not Perfect Phil Tyler, upstanding citizen and family man."

"Tell me, Phoenix," Phil said. He was so weary of this. Maybe it was time he just accepted that there was nothing he could do for Phoenix. That his son was going to have to find his own way out of the anger. "Tell me so I can fix it. I'm tired of arguing with you. And I'm not going to do it any longer. I... have a life of my own I need to live. I'm going to do it now. Whether that upsets you, you're just going to have to man up and deal with it. It's time you learned—the world isn't going to always revolve around what you want. Sometimes you'll have to make the concessions you don't want to. Sometimes things will just be out of your control. And you have to accept that."

"You know what you did."

"No. Honestly, I don't. All I can think is that you are angry with me for that night. For not being the one to drive to go get your sister."

Phoenix flinched as if Phil had struck him. Phil's own eyes narrowed. "That's it. You blame me for your mother dying?"

"I blame Sadie Rutherford. If she hadn't been drunk—"

"Exactly. A drunk driver crossed the center line and killed your mother. She did it. No one else. We all know that."

"Did you? Did you believe me, or Perci, when she told you?" The fury in his son's tone was so hard to miss that Phil almost took a step back.

That's when he got it, when he finally understood. "You are angry with me, and you are angry with yourself. Because Sadie's dead, you can't be angry with her."

"I never would have been driving if Mom hadn't told you to go to bed that night!"

Now Phil was the one who flinched. That was at the heart of it.

For him, too. "I know. And I've lived with that knowledge every single day. And I know every time I look in the mirror that I am the one who killed her. You think you're the only one angry about that night? If I had not put off going to the doctor when your mother asked for months, I would have not been so sick that night. I would have driven in to get your sister. Your mother would be alive. I live with that every single day."

"Dad?" Phoenix just stared at him.

"Then, if that's the case," a quiet voice said from behind them. "Then it's my fault mom's dead."

Both he and Phoenix turned. To see the small woman in hospital scrubs standing there. The back door was open. He had no idea how long she had been standing there, listening. "Honey? It wasn't your fault at all."

"Yes, it was. If I had told someone what Clive was doing to me...my car was working just fine that night," Perci said, tears running down her pretty cheeks. "I was just...it was dark and rainy and cold and *Thursday*, and those were his favorite kind of nights. And I was scared. So I lied. And Mom died because of it."

Phil shook his head as more lights came up his driveway. He and Glenna wouldn't have gotten to have the evening together, after all. Unless he could chase them all away fast. It wasn't even three in the afternoon yet. That was a possibility. "It wasn't your fault. If I had stopped Clive somehow when he was harassing Robin years ago, he wouldn't have even looked in your direction, honey. That was my fault, too."

Phoenix was silent, watching his sister. Phil pulled his baby girl into his arms. "It wasn't your fault, any more than it was your brother's."

"It was Sadie Rutherford's," another voice said. Pip held one of her sons in her arms as she stepped into the kitchen. "Your voices are carrying. Everyone heard everything outside. We... had a minor issue with the electricity at Phoebe's during the repairs. The electrician can't get it back on until morning. Parker wanted to come home. We came home so the guys could help you with the shelves in the basement. Parker and Patton said you were doing the entire back wall today."

Phil winced. He hadn't even thought...he should have. He'd lived in this house for most of his life, after all. "Everyone?"

"Yes," Pip said, compassion and pain in her big blue eyes. "We're all out on the porch. But there is something you need to realize—*no one* is at fault for what happened to Mom except Sadie Rutherford. She chose to drink too much that night, and she chose to drive. What happened to Mom was just...bad luck. Poor circumstances. We, as a family, can't keep seeing you tear yourself up this way, Phoenix. Or you, Dad. You've been trying so hard to be the perfect father since, haven't you?"

As she spoke, the rest of his children filed in. Sons-in-law, too.

Glenna was there on the hall steps. Her cheeks were red as

everyone looked at her. He knew that made her anxious. And everyone knew...what he felt for her.

Phil stepped toward her, reached a hand for her. "I'm sorry you have to see this."

"It's ok." There was compassion in her big green eyes. He acted. Dropped a kiss on her forehead.

One of her small, soft hands covered his. Squeezed. A silent way of her telling him it would be ok. That she was in his corner. He nudged her toward the rocking chair.

Phil pulled in a deep breath and turned to his children, as even Parker filed in.

"What's happening? Daddy?" Parker asked in a worried tone.

"We're figuring a few things out together," Phoebe said, cuddled against Joel's chest, Aria in her arms. They looked so right together. Phil looked at the rest of his girls and their husbands. Nate had scooped Perci right off her feet and snuggled her tight to his chest. Their daughter rested in her uncle Levi's arms, her cousin Griffen in Pan's. The girls got busy, settling their babies down, taking off coats and hats and little boots and mittens and lining them up near the back door.

Where coats and boots and mittens had been placed every winter day since he had first bought the house years ago.

Those little boots meant something to him. Visible symbols of what his life had led to. He was so damned proud of his family he could burst with it.

He wanted to share it...with the woman in the rocking chair trying not to be visible right now. As shy as she was, this was going to be tough for *her* to see.

Pan looked at Phil. "You and Mom taught us years ago to own our mistakes and put things in perspective. To be someone we could look at in the mirror."

"Yes. We did."

"Since we lost her, you've been trying to make up for it by

not allowing yourself to make mistakes," Phoebe said. "You were blaming yourself, weren't you?"

Phil just looked at his kids. His heart. "I don't know. Maybe. Mostly, I was just trying to be there for all of you as best as I could, and still hold...things...together. I'm still not sure I did. I think I just kept faking it until it looked like I made it. When I had the heart attack, I thought, *This is it. I'm going the way my brothers did. I'm leaving my kids behind, too.* And then we found out it was correctible. And...I was angry about that, too. Why could my problem be fixed while your mother's couldn't? Why couldn't my brothers have been saved, too? Losing them all so close together like that—I was afraid I wasn't going to get through those days at all. Why did all of this keep happening? And I felt...I didn't deserve to be the one to pull through. Not...if I hadn't gone to bed early the night your mother died, I would have been driving and not Phoenix. I was a more experienced driver, and to be honest, I would have been *alone*. Getting Perci. If someone was going to die that night, it shouldn't have been your mother. It was my job to protect you, and her, and I let you down." Phil looked at his two youngest boys. "Patton, why don't you take your brother and Ivy into the other room? I'll talk to you and Parker together in a few minutes."

There were some things the kids just didn't need to witness.

His sons didn't like it, but they obeyed, taking Pip's older two with them as well.

"Should *she* really be here?" Phoenix asked with an angry jerk of his head in Glenna's direction. "Shouldn't she take all the babies in the other room and do what you pay her to do? You know, babysit and clean up after everybody?"

She shot a chiding look at Phoenix that said while she was quiet and nonconfrontational, she wasn't cowed—or a pushover. She stared. Phoenix looked away. Glenna looked at

Phil next. "I can go in there with the boys and Ivy." She started to stand.

Phil thought for a moment. This...was for him and his kids to do. It wasn't fair to put her in the middle of it simply because he was nervous of what was going to be said. He nodded. "Can you stay with my boys? I know they are going to be worried. Might hear things through the door they won't understand. Not because Phoenix is lashing out, but..."

Her hand wrapped around his. He used his grip on her to help her fully from the chair.

He pulled her closer. He kissed her, right on the lips. It was as much a declaration for his family as anything could be.

He heard two of his daughters' exclaim. Pan gave a slightly wicked laugh.

"Oh, the irony," his former-housekeeper daughter said.

Glenna looked into Phil's eyes. "We'll talk later if you want."

"I...I'm not sure what I can say." That he was more than sorry their plans had been ruined. That his son wasn't going to be allowed to cheapen what had happened between him and Glenna today.

"I get it, you know." She was close enough to whisper. "I... have my own regrets about what happened to my ex-husband. Like I said, we'll talk later. I'm here to listen."

"Thank you. I mean that. And I'm sorry about him. He...has been so angry since." He cupped her cheeks, just for a moment.

"Of course, he has. I know some of the story. You'll get through this, too."

With that she stepped back. And walked into the living room. He heard her suggest to the kids that they head down-stairs to the new playroom and watch a movie while their dad talked to the others.

He heard Patton's voice, raised in worry, but couldn't distin-guish what he was asking.

That was for later.

Phil turned toward the rest of his children.

"Well. I have one thing to say first." He turned toward his oldest son. "I love you. This will always be your home. But you will not ever speak to someone I have here for any reason in that tone. Do you understand? This is *my* house, and that is one thing I am emphatic about. You will be respectful. Period. No matter how angry you get."

Thirty-Six

THEY WERE ALL LOOKING AT HIM LIKE HE WAS A loser again. Phoenix bit back a curse as the woman left the kitchen.

Maybe he hadn't meant to say what he had in the way he had, and he hadn't meant for her to hear him at all. That had been just...him being a total jerk.

But her stupid bra had been right there, lying next to Pan's normal chair.

Glenna had been all sweet and loving toward his father. She hadn't even glared at Phoenix once. No, when she'd looked at him, she'd looked like she understood.

That threw him, Phoenix would admit to himself.

He didn't want to like her.

She had no business doing anything with his father. The man paid her to clean his toilets. That was all that she should be doing. They had no business screwing around together.

Pan nudged his shoulder. She always had been the one to tell Phoenix off the most. Pan and Perci. "Don't be a jerk to her, Phoenix. We all like her just fine."

Pan shot him a significant look, then shifted the kid in her arms when he fussed. Pan had been Levi's housekeeper. Of course, she'd identify with Glenna or something. They had a lot in common, after all.

Except Glenna was a trauma counselor or something. "Why is she here cleaning toilets if she's a counselor? What's in it for her?"

"She's going to be working with Rhea part-time," Pip said, a snap in her tone that told him he'd screwed up. Pip rarely snapped at anyone at all. If she hadn't been holding her baby now, nursing, she probably would have been on his case, too.

Perci just glared at him. "To build a crisis counseling center. To help with…trauma and mental health. It's a service we need in this county, Phoenix. I think the last several years have just illustrated that. What is your problem with her, really? Her, personally, or the fact that Dad likes her so much? That she's here with him, and you're not?"

When she put it like that, he sounded like a total jackass. Shame hit his cheeks.

"It's not like that. Everybody acts like she's so great. But she's not."

"Oh? Is she hateful? She make Parker eat his brussels sprouts? Is she mean to the kids? The babies? Does she manipulate Dad? What does she do that's so bad?" Pip asked quietly. "You would have a problem with any woman around Dad, Phoenix."

"Girls, let's not let this devolve into a confrontation with Phoenix. He's entitled to his feelings." Phoenix's dad put one hand on his shoulder and squeezed.

Phoenix looked into his dad's face. There was anger there, but mostly, there was pain.

And that made him feel two inches tall. "I get it. No talking bad about your girlfriend while I'm here. Then when I'm gone you can all go back to building your life around Saint Glenna. And I'll be gone."

"You know," his sister Perci's husband said as Pete stood to let the dogs in. "If you'd sit down and shut up and quit acting like a toddler in a tantrum, you might get some answers you can live with."

Phoenix almost said something right back. But who in their right mind got into a fight with a guy that size?

Phoenix wasn't stupid.

And he saw agreement on the rest of their stupid husbands' faces.

On his sisters' faces, too.

Like they were all against him, all over again.

But it was Perci who stopped Phoenix from saying screw them all and storming out. Bodily.

She stepped right in front of him, all five foot two inches of her, with the baby that looked just like her in her arms.

His gaze landed on the scar on her forehead.

He'd never forget looking in the backseat of that stupid car and seeing her covered in blood.

Looking at his mother and seeing her and just knowing she wasn't going to wake up again.

He'd gotten out of the car. Climbed into the back, looking for Perci's bag. He hadn't had a cell phone, then. Only Perci had.

He'd used it to call 911, praying there would be signal that night.

Knowing he'd killed his mother, and terrified he was going to lose Perci, too.

Phoenix could never forget that. He still relived it every night in his dreams.

"We all have regrets about that night." Her pain was right there in her eyes. Perci was the tough one of his sisters. She shouldn't be hurting like this.

Once again, his fault. It was always his fault.

"It wasn't your fault." And it wasn't. It was his. He should have seen the other car.

Sadie Rutherford hadn't bothered to turn her headlights on. She'd just been driving...in the dark. Weaving everywhere.

"It wasn't anyone's fault but Sadie Rutherford's," Joel said. He'd pulled a crying Phoebe into his lap and was comforting her.

Phoenix had never known what to think about this particular brother-in-law. The first time he'd met Joel, he'd tried to slug him. He'd knocked Phoebe down instead.

Phoenix had almost killed her that night, too.

Phoenix had made himself a vow sitting in that stupid jail cell after Joel had arrested him—he was never going to do anything to endanger his sisters again. Or his brothers.

He would find a way to get out of Masterson, and he wouldn't hurt them again.

Rowland said he had talent, too. And he'd taken an interest in Phoenix. Phoenix hoped he could pay the other man back for that someday.

But...he hadn't realized how much of his *family* he would miss out on because of it.

"She chose to drive drunk with her lights off, Phoenix. I don't know how you can keep telling yourself it was your fault." Perci looked at her father. "I've been seeing Rhea's friend. A counselor. She's helped me work through a few things."

She turned back to Phoenix. "I blamed myself, too. For wanting a ride in the first place, for what Clive said and did after, how he refused to believe you had done nothing wrong. How I should have just sucked it up and driven myself—or asked for help. Told everyone what he was doing to me. I've felt guilty for that for a long time."

"Just as Clive wouldn't have been harassing Perci if I hadn't gone outside at that dance. It was irrational, and I know that.

But the thought was there," Pip said. "For a while, I thought that if I hadn't done something to draw Jay's attention—"

"Which I drew *first*, Pip." Perci said. "Don't forget that."

"It sounds to me like there has been way too much blame for everyone," Nate said. "Blame after losing someone is normal, you know. I've felt my share."

Thirty-Seven

PHIL MOTIONED FOR HIS FAMILY TO SETTLE AROUND the table. They'd added more chairs in the last five years.

He liked seeing that. Knowing his family was growing, was going to *keep* growing.

"It's normal. So is the anger," Nate said. "I felt it after my father died at my feet."

"Nate had anger down pat," Perci said. "At least where I was concerned."

"I was angry at myself for letting you get beneath my skin— and not doing anything about it. I was afraid. I'm not too ashamed to admit that. I was afraid of something developing to the same deep level that I saw between my parents. I saw her face when my father died. I'll never forget that moment."

Levi reached out and touched his brother on the shoulder.

"The thing is, grief...makes us think things that just aren't true," Matt added, taking their daughter from Pip. "Part of healing is putting that behind us. Understanding. Moving on. What happened to your mother was no one's fault but the woman who drove drunk and crossed the center line. That it was the three of you out there was just bad circumstances. It could have been anyone. Someone in the wrong place at the wrong time. That's it."

Phil knew they were right, his family. "It doesn't make it easy to let go of."

"No," Perci said. "It doesn't. And it takes time. But we'll all get there eventually. We get a little closer every day. I like Glenna a lot, by the way. I think she fits you. The *you* you are now, not the man you were five years ago. Although that man was a good man, too."

"Me, too," Phil said. This was not how he'd ever intended to tell his kids. "Listen, I don't know what will happen between us. Her job may eventually become full-time. Rhea has already spoken with her about it. She might want to move closer to town. Robin is moving back, too. She and Glenna are extremely close. She might want to live in town near Robin and the kids. I just know that…the world looks a little brighter when I'm with her. I feel brighter. Younger. Alive again. I kind of lost that over the last few years."

He had felt *alive* with that woman today. And he didn't just mean the making love. No. It had been more than that.

Phil felt like he had found *home* again.

"So everything is just going to fall into place perfectly?" Phoenix asked. "Like mom never existed."

"Now that's just being stupid," Pan said hotly. She and Phoenix always had tangled the most. "Let's be realistic here. Look at us. Look at what, who, Mom left behind, Phoenix. Eight kids and seven grandkids already. People who will remember her and look like her forever. Do you think she would want Dad to go through life alone, just a caretaker for the rest of us? Hell, no. She'd want him out there finding someone to *love*. Just like she would have been beyond thrilled to have met Levi and his brothers. There is no way I would want Levi to spend the rest of *his* life alone, if something happens to me."

The rest of the girls nodded in total agreement. Pip stood, moved right in front of her younger brother. Until he was looking at her. She spoke in her quiet voice that always resonated so much. "Now you're being selfish. Consumed with how everything made you feel. You've wrapped your cloak of pain around you so tight you can't see that it's time to throw it off and actually live in the world again. We aren't going to wallow in it with you, even though we definitely understand it. We all know what it was like back then. We'll never forget it. I'd like to think it means we can appreciate what comes next so much more."

Phil listened to his daughter's words and knew she spoke the utter truth. "Your mother wouldn't have wanted any of us to not have *love*."

"Fine then. You've all figured it out. I'm going...back to town. I just...hope everything works out perfectly for all of you."

Just like that, his son stormed out of the house again. Like he had so many times before.

Phil took a step after him. Stopped.

Phoenix was twenty-two years old. At that age, Phil had a baby on the way, a wife to support, and a ramshackle cabin on the corner of his dad's property. They'd added four more kids before they had been able to move out of that two-bedroom place into this one. It hadn't been much of a step up, considering the shape this place had been in then. It had just been bigger. With more problems to fix. But he had fixed them.

He had built it into something he could be proud of. Him and Becky both. The fruit of his labors surrounded him now.

It hadn't been easy.

He'd been angry and terrified and worried more often than not. But he'd put on his big boy boots and stepped his rear out into the snow when it was snowing, out in the rain when it was raining, and out in the heat when it was scorching.

To do what had to be done.

Because he had a responsibility to the ones he loved.

A responsibility to himself to be the kind of man he wanted to be. The kind of man he was raising his sons to be.

Phoenix...it was time he figured a few things out on his own.

Apparently, Phoenix wasn't ready for that just yet.

But Phil had faith that he would be. When it was time.

He turned back to his daughters.

It was time they all had a serious talk.

Then he would make dinner. Give Glenna some time to herself tonight. Let her find her balance after *this*.

Because come tomorrow, he had plans to make. Plans that involved her.

Phil looked at his daughters and their husbands, at the *love* they had between them.

He wanted that again. That intrinsic connection that was so strong between his girls and their husbands that it was almost visible.

And he wanted it with Glenna.

Phil considered himself a man of action—when he had a plan, he stuck to it. Now he had to figure out how to make what he wanted with Glenna happen.

Thirty-Eight

PHOENIX HAD CALLED ONCE IN THE THREE WEEKS since he had stormed out of the house after Phil and Glenna had been together.

That call hadn't gone as well as Phil would have liked. Phoenix hadn't called since.

Worry for his son was the only blight on his horizon right now.

Things had changed after that night. For him and Glenna especially. They hadn't had a chance to be together again, not in the way he so wanted. The kids and the ranch had kept them both hopping in different directions.

As had Rhea Masterson. Somehow, Phil had been recruited to help with preparing the building Rhea had bought to use as her mental health clinic. She was picking his brain at the oddest times of the day about what he knew about W4HAV. Or ordering him around with the repairs he somehow ended up helping his nephews Martin, Michael, Chandler, Reese, and Kaece make. And whoever else Rhea could recruit.

Rhea kept stealing Glenna away from him and the kids whenever she could manage it. Glenna was spending half her days with Rhea—and Phil's niece Maggie and niece-by-marriage Jude—getting the facility planned and started.

Glenna came home tired but with a gleam of satisfaction and purpose in her beautiful green eyes. Phil loved to see it— even if it meant he was responsible for six kids instead of his three when she was gone.

He didn't mind for one minute. He was kept busy with the calves and with feeding livestock during part of the day, but Pete watched the kids then. Or one of his daughters. Someone was always there to help Glenna, it seemed. Without her asking.

Almost as if his daughters had coordinated it between them.

He strongly suspected they had.

Everyone was pulling together like a team. Just like he wanted to see.

Everything felt...easy. Right. Good.

If he was worried about Phoenix, that was nothing really new. He had almost always worried about that boy. Phil tried not to let it eat at him. But sometimes, sometimes it just happened.

Phoenix had been on his mind a lot today. He had rarely gone a week without calling home, checking in.

He thought about his son as he finished picking up the signs of seven grandchildren who'd stopped by to visit for the afternoon, mingled with the signs of four kids under the age of eleven and two teenagers that lived in his own house.

It brought an odd sort of satisfaction, seeing his house that had provided so much love and shelter to so many kids through the years put back together again. Waiting for the next day. When it would all start over again.

He loved this place. Loved the people in it more.

Phil was *happy*. Bone-deep happy again. Like he hadn't felt in five years.

He straightened as that sank in.

He would *always* miss Becky and hurt for her loss. They had intended to grow old together. Had wanted to rock those grandchildren side by side. That wasn't what fate had in store for him, them. He'd accepted that now.

But he had room in his life to have more than he had since he had lost her.

He still had life left in him.

Becky wouldn't want him to miss out on growing old with someone. She'd want him happy. More than anything, that woman would have wanted him and their children *happy*.

Even if it meant he was happy with another woman.

Phil wanted Phoenix to find what made him happy. He couldn't do that for his son. He had to trust that Phoenix could find it in his own time, his own way.

The kitchen door pushed open. A woman stood there, bags of groceries in her arms, and a pink hat on her head. She'd been stolen away by Rhea again. He was glad she was home. The sky had been darkening all afternoon, and he'd started to worry. Had thought about calling her and telling her to stay where she was, that he was coming in to get her.

Another late season storm was on its way in now. It was going to be a bad one, from what the reports were saying. He'd wanted Glenna home, where she belonged. Safe with him and the kids who loved her so much.

"The grocery store was insane. I just went for those cookies Parker and Emmy like so much. Came out with all of this. I practically had to fight my way through the chicken nuggets."

"It's because of the weather report. People have to get their bread, milk, and eggs. Every time." Phil walked up to her and took the groceries. Put them on the counter. He didn't say another word.

Just unzipped her royal-blue coat and slipped it from her shoulders.

He scooped her close, only vaguely aware of the herd of kids rushing into the kitchen to greet her.

He had seen her first. She was his for the moment. The kids would just have to wait.

Startled green eyes stared into his. "Hi."

"Shhh. I've missed you today, woman. Give me a kiss." Phil knew he was probably rushing things a bit, overstepping certainly. They had kept things a bit on the quiet side in front of the younger kids. She was worried it would just confuse the younger four until they had things figured out completely between them. He had had to agree. The last thing either of them wanted to do was cause problems for the kids. But today...

Phil was happy.

Because of her.

"Gross! Hope you used breath mints!" Parker yelled, but he was laughing. Evey was making gagging noises. Emmy and Elly were already tugging on Glenna's sweater, wanting their mother's attention.

Phil kissed Glenna quickly, then pulled back. Checked their kids. Even Pete stood in the doorway. But there was an approving look on his boy's face. He had taken to Glenna quickly, too. All of his kids had—except for Phoenix.

He stepped back, lifted Elly into his arms when she demanded it. Then she was reaching for her mother with one tiny hand. "Again! Kiss again!"

Glenna just laughed, reached up. Toward *him*. Phil took advantage of the situation and dropped another kiss on her lips. Then he kissed the little girl on the forehead with an exaggerated smacking noise. Stepped back, lifted Emmy and did the same to her. "Come on, kids, let's get the groceries put away. Then we'll figure out what we're going to do for dinner. Anyone want pizza?"

That was a given.

Yes. Phil was finally happy again. He slipped his arm around Glenna's waist and just pulled her closer.

She looked up at him, a question in those eyes of hers. "You make me happy, Glenna Carnes. I'm glad I found you down there in Finley Creek and brought you home with me. Where you belong."

Her cheeks reddened. "Me, too."

Thirty-Nine

No one had even noticed he was there. Phoenix stood in his father's back door and watched his father kissing the housekeeper.

Phoenix hadn't called first. Rowland had called him into his office that morning and ordered him to fly home. To work on the project Hunter Clark had had going on with Phoenix's cousin Nikki. Rowland wanted real progress since Hunter had had to cut it short.

Rowland couldn't seem to get ahold of Nikki easily enough for him to get his questions answered.

Jenny, Rowland's favorite assistant, had told Phoenix privately she thought Nikki was avoiding all calls from L.A. right now. Phoenix had also been ordered to check on Nikki, make sure she was doing ok.

Rowland was worried. Extremely so.

Said Nikki had been in love with Hunter. Hunter's leaving had apparently devastated her.

Phoenix thought that was stupid; Nikki wouldn't have done something that crazy. She had to have known nothing permanent could have come from a fling with Hunter.

Not Nikki, she was far smarter, far more practical than that. And if she had, well, Phoenix was going to kick Hunter's ass for hurting her, first chance Phoenix got.

Phoenix hadn't seen Nikki yet. He had plans to go over to her bookstore in the morning. He'd driven by there tonight, but she'd already closed for the day. He hadn't seen any lights on in her apartment either.

Maybe she'd taken off with one of her friends or something.

Nikki was always involved in something, doing something. She rarely stayed home. She was the true social butterfly of the Tyler clan.

He would find her in the morning.

Rowland just wanted a status update, mostly. And he had wanted someone to actually *see* Nikki, too. Rowland was a bit overprotective of the women he cared about. Since he'd saved her life two and a half years ago, that included Nikki. Even if Rowland would never come out and say that aloud.

Here he was, Rowland Bowles's errand boy.

He hadn't truly minded. Phoenix had really been missing home these past couple of weeks. He'd had things he wanted to talk to his dad about, anyway. There was an acting academy he was thinking of taking a few classes at.

Rowland was pushing him to consider acting for a living. He'd even offered to pay for the classes for Phoenix. Well, Phoenix was a Tyler—they didn't take charity well. But Rowland was pushing. Saying he could make Phoenix as big as Hunter Louis Clark someday.

Probably a bad idea to mention Clark to Phoenix if the man truly had taken advantage of Phoenix's cousin and just dropped her cold like that.

Phoenix just wanted to talk to his dad. Get his opinion on what Phoenix's future should look like.

Well, apparently, that wasn't going to happen tonight either. Not with *her* and her kids around, too.

"Well, see things haven't changed much here. Still kissing Glenna."

Even he heard the asshole quality in his words now.

"Phoenix! You're back," his dad said. But he didn't step away from Glenna. Instead, his arms tightened around her and her middle girl. And he shot a warning look right at Phoenix.

One that told Phoenix everything he needed to know.

His dad had fallen for her even more, was going to build a perfect life with her and the kids. All roses and kisses and kittens or something.

"Yeah, Rowland had some questions for Nikki about that project Hunter Clark was working on. He sent me back today."

"We're ordering pizza tonight," Pete said. There was a warning look on his brother's face. One that told Phoenix Pete was ready to kick his ass if he didn't toe the line.

That Pete meant it, too. And thought he could.

Phoenix really looked at the brother closest to him in age for once.

Phoenix almost didn't recognize the guy staring back at him.

Pete was two inches taller than Phoenix's six two and fifty pounds heavier. Muscled. His younger brother might actually be able to accomplish kicking Phoenix's ass now. Easily.

When he'd left Masterson two years ago, Pete had been five eight or so and scrawny. A kid.

Pete was practically a man now.

When had that happened?

His dad finally moved away from his precious Glenna. Parker stepped in front of her protectively. Wrapped his arms around her waist and hugged her, shooting a hateful look at Phoenix as he did so. Even Patton had a worried look on his face as he stared at Phoenix. Glenna's three girls just watched him out of eyes as green as Glenna's, apprehension on their tiny faces, little blond ponytails sticking out everywhere.

And Glenna, just standing there, still in her boots. Watching him calmly. Waiting for him to say something only a total jackass would say?

Did they all think he was a monster or something?

"Shut the door, Phoenix. You're letting all the heat out," his dad said. Phoenix obeyed. His dad wrapped him in a quick hug. "Glad you're back. Now we have even more to celebrate. Missed you, son. Welcome home."

That was part of the problem. Phoenix wasn't certain this was his home any longer.

Forty

PHOENIX NEEDED TIME TO THINK. HE'D GONE BACK to the inn, where he had a room courtesy of Rowland Bowles. He could have stayed at his dad's, but that was the last place he really wanted to be right now.

But he couldn't stay at the inn either. It felt too...impersonal. He'd spent the evening with his family, watching his brothers and those little girls act like...Phoenix and Pete and Patton and Parker used to with Phoebe, Pip, Perci, and Pan.

His dad had treated those little girls like they were *his*. And Glenna, well, she treated his brothers like their mother used to. She'd listened to them, included them, acted like she wanted to be with them.

And she and his dad had acted like they'd been married for fifty years already.

They had all acted like they were...a family.

One that didn't really include *him*.

Even Perci had called while they were waiting for dinner to arrive. To see if Glenna and Phoenix's dad could watch Ivy and Poppy overnight while she and Nate went to a medical conference in Cheyanne the following weekend.

She'd asked *Glenna* while Phoenix's dad was busy with the kids. She and his dad had discussed it together. Like they were a unit, a team now.

That had really thrown Phoenix off.

He needed to talk to his dad again. Get a few of the questions still in his head answered—about Glenna...and about his own life. Maybe it was time he stopped running away from the hard questions in life? Make his own decisions.

Started *being* the kind of man he wanted to be.

Hell. He wanted to *be* the kind of man his father was. The kind of men his uncles were.

But he had no idea how he was supposed to do that.

He didn't like knowing everyone had looked at him like he was being a stupid jerk kid again tonight when he'd first gotten there.

He hadn't said much tonight, but he hadn't been rude either.

Looking back, he had been acting like a total asshole a month ago.

Mad because his dad had a new girlfriend. That was kid's stuff. Something Parker would do and feel.

He climbed into his rental truck. He would check in with his dad again, tell him Phoenix was sorry for being an idiot. And maybe...he'd apologize to Glenna, too.

He really had been a rude asshole to her, and he didn't even know her at all.

Phoenix didn't like the man he was becoming.

He thought about that as he started the engine of the rental. It had all the bells and whistles, courtesy of Rowland Bowles Studios.

It was better than any truck his father had ever owned. But Phoenix didn't feel like they'd ever gone without anything that truly mattered. Food might have not been falling out of the cabinets overflowing like it was *now*, but they'd had what they really needed when they needed it.

Because of his dad and his mom.

And after they'd lost their mother, because of his dad and Phoenix's sisters. He'd never forget how he'd feel every night when Perci would come in at three a.m. exhausted after working a double shift at the hospital just to help support the rest of them. To buy groceries.

Nothing Phoenix had done had made it better.

Until he'd just stopped trying and just started *fighting*.

There was nothing he was ashamed of more.

He wouldn't ever go hungry now. He put back a part of his paycheck into savings every week.

And if it ever came to it, he'd see to it that Parker and Patton and Pete never went hungry, either. Or any of his nieces and nephews.

If that meant coming back to Masterson and working two shifts at a stupid factory, he would do it.

He would do what he had to do for the people he loved. Without hesitating. No question. They were his family, and he loved them.

Maybe it had been the same for his sisters?

They'd worked themselves exhausted because they loved the rest of the family, too? Pan had cleaned people's toilets for money until she'd been hired by Levi—to clean *his* toilets—and had moved into his house then.

Phoenix snorted at that. Yeah, right, she'd been hired to clean Levi's toilets. No. The guy had been hot for Pan, and he'd manipulated her to get her into his bed, where he'd truly wanted her.

Levi had just married her after.

Phoenix believed they loved each other now. It was in the way Levi practically drooled all over her. They even had a baby now. A family.

Pan was happy. It was written all over her.

For a moment, he wondered what that felt like. Being a parent. Being responsible for a completely defenseless human being.

He didn't know if he'd ever be ready for that. If he would ever be able to *keep* someone else he loved safe.

He hadn't been able to protect his mother. Or Perci. Or Pan and Pip and Phoebe when it came down to it.

He had failed in just about everything he'd ever tried. Except working for Rowland. He was terrified if he did this acting thing, he'd fail at that, too. Then where would he be?

Phoenix was thinking about that and what it meant about him and about how he really felt about his dad's new girlfriend.

Maybe she wasn't that bad. Just because his dad had a thing for her didn't mean he was going to go all stupid and marry her.

Then again, maybe he would. His dad wasn't the kind of guy to get involved with a woman unless he *meant* it. He'd raised Phoenix to be the exact same way.

Maybe his dad would marry Glenna, adopt her little girls or something. Go from eight kids to eleven.

He bet that would make his dad happy. Like he had seemed tonight, rocking that littlest girl while Glenna had been busy with Parker.

It probably really would make his dad happy. Getting three more kids like that.

His dad felt special being a dad. He took a lot of pride in being a father.

Phoenix wasn't too stupid to see that.

Maybe that wasn't a bad thing?

Making certain the kids you loved knew you would always be there for them. No matter what they did.

Phoenix just didn't know if he felt like his father had been there like that for *him*.

He was so caught up in his thoughts he didn't see the crowd forming ahead at first. When he realized who it was, he cursed—the sheriff's truck was distinctive, as was his brother-in-law Matt's truck with *Masterson Vet Clinic* on the side.

That was his family out there, and that truck was in the damned ditch now. *Pip* and their three kids could have been in that truck. Terror filled Phoenix in an instant. Something could have happened to his sister. Those kids. Even Matt, the quietest of his brothers-in-law.

Someone from his family could be hurt.

If Phoenix was out there, he was damned well going to help.

He was a Tyler, and Tylers took care of Tylers, after all.

Phoenix pulled the rental truck up behind the sheriff's and climbed out.

Forty-One

GLENNA WAS UPSTAIRS, GETTING THE GIRLS' FRESHLY washed sheets on the bed. Dinner had been better than expected; Phoenix hadn't said much, but he hadn't been insulting and rude either.

Phil had gotten the feeling Phoenix had something important on his mind he hadn't been ready to share yet.

But tonight wasn't for thoughts of Phoenix. That was for tomorrow.

He had something else to deal with tonight. Phil and Glenna needed to have a serious talk.

He didn't want her thinking he had expectations of her that she wasn't ready or prepared to make, of more with her than she was ready to give. That was the last thing he wanted.

He wanted her to know he wasn't ever going to do anything to rush her.

And he felt he needed to explain Phoenix and what was eating at that boy's heels.

She wasn't upstairs. Phil kept looking. He found the woman he wanted in the kitchen, wiping down the counters.

A few moments of quiet, finally.

Her hair was up in a sweet ponytail that made his fingers itch to touch. He heard the sounds of the wind picking up outside.

Tonight would be the perfect night for them to curl up together on the couch—and just talk.

He wanted that more than he wanted anything right now. Glenna in his arms while the house was quiet and calm, the storm raging around outside.

Phil shot a look toward the living room. He could see one of the boys' feet on the footstool in front of Phil's favorite chair. He could hear the sounds of a kids' movie playing on the TV.

They were good for now. He checked the clock. Glenna's younger two would be going to bed in about half an hour. He maybe had ten minutes before she had to go start the pre-bedtime routine.

Then his boys stayed up ninety minutes later, her eldest would have an extra half an hour after her sisters.

Then...then Glenna was his.

But for now, Phil slipped up behind her and wrapped his hands around her waist.

She jumped a bit, then turned. Gave him the sweetest smile that shot straight to his gut. "Hi. Everything taken care of out there?"

"Yep. I was able to beat the storm. Everything peaceful in here?"

"Hmmm. Elly's a little fussy and whiny. And very cranky. I'm not certain, but I think the ear infection is returning. I may need to talk to the pediatrician about tubes. But I'm keeping an eye on her. Everyone else is good. They were a bit wound up from the soda with the pizza, but I think they're settled now." She turned in his arms. Just like that, he backed his house-keeper up against the counter and just *felt* her against him.

Phil wanted to scoop her up into his arms and carry her off to his lair. Show her what she meant to him again.

But he'd have to settled for words this time. "How about we send them all to their beds, lock them in, and just enjoy each other?"

She laughed. "I don't think it quite works that way."

"I wish it did. I...this ponytail thing, it tempts a man to touch, you know."

"Really? It just seems so practical, with the kids, and..." Her hand slipped up over his chest.

He wanted to lean forward and just breathe the woman in.

If he could touch her like this every day for the rest of his life, Phil thought he might just end up ok, after all.

He started to tell her that, when the phone rang.

Phil grabbed it. Listened to the frantic words of his second daughter. "I'm on my way."

He disconnected. Turned to Glenna. "Keep the kids inside, no matter what. The dogs, too. Nikki's...been in an accident. She's lost in the woods between here and Wreck Curve Road. I'm going out to look for her now."

He was out of the house in less than five minutes, fear for his niece taking precedence over everything else now.

When he caught up with three of his sons-in-law on the road less than a quarter of a mile from where his wife had died, the fear just tripled.

Nikki was as defenseless as a person could be right now. And in this cold, the approaching storm, Phil didn't know if they'd be able to find her in time.

Forty-Two

PHOENIX FOUGHT THE FEAR AS HE LISTENED TO instructions from his brother-in-law Joel on what to do next. They were splitting into two groups. Half were going to head over to the service road that led to his dad's place and a few others, including his uncle Bill's, on East Tyler Road. The other half would approach from Wreck Curve Road. They were going to spread out and start through the woods in the middle of a damned storm and hope they found Nikki along the way.

Nikki was out there somewhere.

They'd found her glasses broken in the snow.

Nikki was legally blind without her glasses.

She couldn't see where she was going, she'd been in a car accident, it was getting darker and darker out, the storm was coming in fast, and it was damned cold right now.

If they didn't find her soon, there wouldn't be any hope for her at all.

Nikki was two years older than Phoenix. Young. She still had her entire future ahead of her. She couldn't be lost like this.

Because of bad luck. Circumstances.

Nikki hadn't done *anything* to deserve this. She'd just been unlucky.

Phoenix's gaze landed on the wooden crosses along Wreck Curve Road.

One of those crosses was his mother's.

But there were more than just hers there.

More people had been in the wrong place at the wrong times than just his mother.

They probably hadn't been able to control it—any more than Nikki had been able to control *this* tonight.

Phoenix just kept trudging through the snow, calling his cousin's name, and hoping.

Movement to his left caught his attention, and he jerked. Seeing the two men there, *some* of his fear lessened. His dad. His uncle Nick. With large flashlights and rifles. Steady and stable and able to handle anything the world threw at them tonight.

And so could Phoenix. He was a man now. Needed. No matter what they found out there in the snow on Tyler Road.

Forty-Three

PHIL ESTIMATED THEY'D ONLY BEEN COMBING THE woods for ten minutes when he heard shouting. A scream. What he recognized easily enough as a gunshot. Phil hurried through the snow and woods as fast as he could with the snow up to his knees.

He put himself in front of Phoenix instinctively. If there was shooting out there, he would be between it and his son. No matter what.

"It came from that way!" Someone shouted. He thought it was his nephew Fletcher, but it was hard to tell in the approaching darkness and the heavy cold weather gear.

Fletcher—Nikki's brother. He was just one of almost two dozen people searching now.

There were *Tylers* in the woods now. That was damned reassuring. They would find Nikki. None of them would give up until they did.

They came to a small clearing, no more than thirty by thirty.

There were other men coming up. And a beautiful young woman rolling to her side. In the damned falling snow.

Phil reached Nikki's side just as Nate came into the clearing. "Nate! Over here."

Phil leaned down and helped her the rest of the way to her feet. She was already trying to get up.

She was moving.

Thank God.

Phil helped get his niece to the waiting trucks a quarter of a mile away.

He held the girl close to his chest, trying to keep her warm, the entire way to the hospital. Just telling her everyone was going to be all right now. Phil just held Nikki close and told her that he loved her.

He hadn't thought they'd find her in time. Nikki was as dear to him as one of his own girls. And they could have lost her so easily.

Just how...capricious fate could be wasn't lost on him tonight.

When he got home, he was going to sit Glenna down and tell her that. Tell her he wasn't ever going to be ready to let her go. That time was too short for them to waste even a minute of it.

Not one minute more. He wasn't going to waste another moment with the woman he loved, ever again.

Forty-Four

PHOENIX STAYED OUT ON THE SCENE, AS JOEL called it.

Nikki wouldn't hurt a fly.

She hadn't deserved this at all.

Slater Davis, a guy Phoenix knew from L.A. who'd been in the movie filmed on his dad's place three years ago, needed a ride to the hospital, too. He ended up being hauled off in the same truck as Hunter Clark.

It was a very real possibility he had frostbite on his hands and feet after all of this.

Phoenix wasn't even certain why Slater Davis was *there*. Slater hadn't hesitated to help Nikki, no matter what it meant for him.

Maybe Slater wasn't such an asshole, after all.

Joel put a hand on his back. "Can you give Gil a ride in a few minutes? Fletcher took Nikki in his truck, along with your dad. Levi and Matt are going to see to it your dad's truck gets back to his place. We'll need to photograph the scene and do some documenting, that kind of thing. Same with that guy's rental. The rest of your cousins and uncles are on their way to the hospital to see how Nikki is doing. Gil's anxious to get there himself."

His cousin Gil had headed back up to his own place to grab a tractor with a hitch. They were going to have to get the trucks off the highway soon. His cousins Monroe and Reese and Kaece had arrived and were already discussing how to make it happen with Monroe's tow truck—once Joel gave the all clear.

Phoenix stood where he was for a moment and actually *saw* the men around him for what they were—women, too. Like it was the first time he was seeing them.

That FBI agent who was the granddaughter of the woman who owned the diner and the police deputy Sage Lowell were out there, too. They'd been a part of the search team. He actually *saw* them.

Competent, strong, doing what they had to do. Even though they'd all dealt with some seriously shitty things, too. Reece and Kaece had lost both of their parents in a flood. That FBI agent's mom had died from cancer when she'd been a kid. Fletcher, Gil, Ben, and Nikki's dad had had a heart attack five years ago. Their mother had died almost six years before that from some sort of bacterial infection they just couldn't treat.

None of them had had it perfect and fine.

Yet there they were. Doing what they had to do.

He wondered if their ghosts ever haunted *them*.

Forty-Five

GLENNA SAW THE WORRY IN THE BOYS' EYES. PETE wanted to join his dad out there. She wasn't about to let that happen. Every horror story she'd ever heard about people getting lost in the woods ran through her head as she moved the girls through their pre-bedtime routines and then spoke quietly with the three boys.

Sticking to the routine was the best option for the kids right now.

Worry for Phil and his niece, and whoever else was out there, about drove her crazy.

Pete, usually calm and steady, was more agitated than she had ever seen him, too. He looked a great deal like his father as he paced around the kitchen. That touched something in her.

Glenna stopped him at one point and hugged him. "Your dad and uncles will find her. I'm sure of that."

"I just don't know why this stuff keeps happening to us." There...there was the kid that was still inside of him. Searching for understanding one of his years just couldn't have yet. Glenna understood that hurt. That confusion.

But she knew...that understanding could really only come with *time*.

"Pete, bad things happen to all of us. It's how we get through them that matters." She resisted looking toward the door. Where Phil was. He was out there, somewhere. "You just lean on your family, give yourself time to heal, to grieve if needed, and you do your best to go on."

She resisted looking toward the door for the four hundredth time. She wanted Phil home.

He was out there, with a sweet young woman Glenna had liked very much. She prayed that girl wasn't going to be a victim of the storm. That Phil and his family wouldn't lose someone else they loved tonight.

Pete hugged her back, even though he had to feel he was a bit too old for that. Patton stayed close to her, even after she put the girls to bed.

He really was a sensitive child.

She wished she could just wrap him up, too, but at four-teen, he definitely wouldn't let her do that.

Parker, though, he hugged her tighter than ever before.

She didn't quite know how to answer his questions tonight either.

But then again, the question of *why* these kinds of things happened was a question no one could ever truly answer.

She was worried sick about Phil out there. Anything... anything could happen to anyone. She hugged his youngest son close for one extra hug before telling him good night. Telling him that she loved him, too, when he said it to her for the first time.

She meant it, too. She loved these sons of Phil's. So very much.

Then she settled in the living room to wait.

She was still there an hour later when Phil called to tell her to send the boys on to bed, if they were still up. That Nikki had been found. And was going to be just fine.

She told Pete and Patton that, and sent them to bed.

After they were upstairs, she sat there and cried. She'd heard the hurt in Phil's voice tonight.

When he'd told her he loved her over the phone. She'd heard the meaning in his words. Heard the truth.

Life was too short to not seize every moment of it that she could.

What that meant for *her*, Glenna hadn't quite figured that part out yet. Glenna sat there in the rocking chair in the kitchen and tried to decide just what that was. When her youngest called out for her, fussy and feverish again, Glenna settled Elly into her lap and just held her. Rocked.

And waited.

Forty-Six

PHOENIX STARED AT THE LIGHT IN HIS FATHER'S kitchen window, debating whether he should take that next step inside.

Tonight...had changed him. That he couldn't deny. He just wasn't sure how.

His cousin Nikki had almost died tonight—because one man couldn't respect that another wanted to be *loved*.

That Hunter wanted to love Nikki in return.

Nikki and Hunter had gotten lucky to be rescued in time. They could have frozen to death out there so easily. Hunter had been out there, searching the woods for the woman he loved.

Because someone was jealous of Hunter's love for Nikki.

Nikki, who had never hurt anyone before in her life.

Phoenix didn't understand it any more than he understood what had happened to his sisters. How could someone let anger and bitterness and hurt cause them to almost kill an innocent woman like Nikki?

He couldn't stay out there forever. His dad had ridden in with Nikki to the hospital.

Probably to help keep the rest of Phoenix's cousins under

control in the hospital waiting room. Tylers had a reputation, after all.

But so did Phoenix's brother-in-law Nate. If they got too rowdy, Nate would toss them out on their ears.

Maybe that would be needed. Maybe it wouldn't.

He took that first step up to the back door. Slipped his key into the lock.

Pushed his way inside, quietly.

Pete had a spare bed in his room now. Phoenix would just crash there for the night, then head back to L.A. in the morning. There was going to be a real storm once the world got ahold of what had happened with Hunter Louis Clark and Slater Davis in Masterson. Phoenix would be needed to help Rowland's favorite personal assistant Jenny handle everything.

Phoenix wasn't needed *here* anymore. It was hard to not let the anger that caused devour him. He was so tired of anger and bitterness. Seeing what happened tonight had just made that so much clearer.

He'd recognized his problem with Glenna out there in the frozen woods tonight.

He was jealous of the fact that she *fit* with his family, and he didn't feel like he did any longer.

Not since the night they'd lost his mother.

Jealousy had almost cost Nikki her life.

He didn't want to be like the man who had hurt her. Jealous and bitter and angry. He couldn't live like that any longer.

He stepped into his father's kitchen. And stopped.

As if his thoughts had worked against him, conjured her, or something...there she was.

There, rocking one of her daughters in his mother's old wooden rocking chair, was *Glenna*.

She had a wide-eyed look on her pretty face. She really was a good-looking woman, attractive. She had that shy air about her, similar to Pip, at times. But men would look at her. His dad certainly had.

"Phoenix! Is your dad with you?" She shot a look behind him. One filled with nerves.

And fear.

This woman was afraid of him. Seriously afraid to be almost alone with him. Phoenix felt like a damned toad. "No. He rode to the hospital with them. I don't know when he'll be back."

"Is everyone ok?" She had one hand over her daughter's head like she was protecting the little girl from the threat in the room. And that threat was Phoenix.

"Yeah, for the most part. Nikki was a bit beat up. And her boyfriend was shot, but he'll be ok."

Those green eyes widened. "I thought it was a car accident!"

Phoenix slipped his coat free and hung it on the far peg by the back door. The one reserved for guests. His usual spot had a little pink coat with *ruffles* on it hanging proudly. One of Glenna's girls, of course.

There were six coats hanging on the kids' hooks now: Pete, Patton, Parker, and Glenna's girls. Like Phoenix and his four sisters hadn't ever existed. Mattered.

But that was just stupid. They'd mattered—they'd just moved to the next step in life. The next phase.

They'd left childhood behind. Had kids of their own. They didn't *need* special coat hooks at his dad's any longer.

Coat hooks. Something so simple made things so clear.

"Not really. Hunter's friend was jealous over Nikki and decided to kill her so Hunter would go back to L.A."

Glenna's eyes widened.

"But Hunter got to her in time." The guy had beaten Nikki's attacker to within an inch of his life. Phoenix couldn't blame Hunter. If he had gotten to the guy first, he'd have started swinging, too. Without her glasses, Nikki hadn't had much hope out there tonight. Everyone had known that.

She'd been almost as defenseless...as the little girl currently sleeping on Glenna's shoulder.

He remembered his mom rocking him like that. He vaguely wondered if Parker remembered that, too. Parker had only been five when they'd lost her. His sisters had tried to step in, give him a *mother*, but...they were sisters. Not Parker's mother.

It didn't seem possible that it had been five years already. Parker had almost been without a mother longer than he'd ever had one. That seriously sucked for his baby brother.

Glenna probably was a *good* mom.

Parker wouldn't remember how good *their* mom had been. The kid had been robbed of that.

Phoenix had stood at that kitchen counter making brownies with *his* mom. Parker wouldn't remember doing that. But maybe...he would get to remember making them with Glenna. Maybe she would be enough of a mother for Parker for the next eight years, instead? His brother did deserve that, didn't he?

"Thank God she's safe."

"Yeah."

They stared at each other for a long while, the only sound in the room the creaking the old rocking chair made on the linoleum floor and a tiny girl's sniffles in her sleep.

Finally, it was Glenna that spoke.

"I'm not trying to replace her, you know."

He wasn't ready for a confrontation between them tonight, but he suspected that was where this was headed. "My dad is paying you to do just that."

"Your dad is paying me to help him be the best parent *he* can be. His time is so limited with your brothers. If by doing the laundry and dishes I can help with that, I am glad to do it." She straightened the blanket over the little girl's back. Phoenix was ashamed to say he didn't remember the kid's name. She was sleeping in his dad's house, and he didn't even know her name. "Your dad...swooped in and rescued me in a moment I desperately needed it. He was there when I needed him most."

"He has a thing for you." A part of Phoenix was convinced she'd done it on purpose. Made his dad fall for her. Tricked him or something. Why else would everything change so quickly? Phoenix had fallen for that girl in L.A. that fast. Only to learn she'd been using *him*. He didn't want some woman using his dad that way.

Of course, his dad wasn't stupid enough to fall for that. Not like Phoenix had been, anyway.

"Yes. And I have a thing for him. I admitted that to myself tonight. I have…a real… *thing*…for your father. But it's *him* I'm going to tell how I feel first. Not you. I never expected to feel this way. Not after my divorce. That terrifies me, honestly. I…never would have moved into his house if Robin hadn't insisted it was a good idea. If Lacy Deane hadn't told me the girls would be safe. I never expected there to be more feelings between us than that. Feelings…complicate things in a way I'm not sure I know how to handle."

Well, he could understand that. "You could always leave."

"I could. I'm not a young girl, Phoenix. I know what I am capable of, and I can take care of myself—and my children. I am going to be working with Rhea Masterson and Jude to build a mental health center in Masterson. It's going to be part-time. I could get another part-time job, even with the hospital, if I need to. I don't want to. The girls are settling in here. Enjoying living here. I don't want to disrupt them if I don't have to."

She shot another level look at him, but he didn't miss the way her hands trembled. He was still scaring her. And she was confronting her fear—with him. "And I'm not going to just because *you* don't want me near your father. That's not fair to any of us, to give you that kind of power over *our* futures. No one has the power over another's life like that. We both are old enough to understand that."

It wasn't. Phoenix couldn't deny that. But a man had his pride. He just shrugged. There were brownies on a platter in the middle of the table. He helped himself to one.

"Parker made those tonight. He was very proud of himself. He did a good job, and it took his mind off of Nikki. He was very worried for your cousin. He takes being a part of your family very seriously. He told me several times that Tylers take care of Tylers tonight."

"I'll tell him they are really good."

"He really looks up to you. You're all he talks about. You...and that Hollywood producer. You are his hero."

"I don't feel like anyone's hero." The words slipped out before he could stop them. "Even tonight, I was pretty useless. Just another body in the snow."

They'd formed a circle. And just kept walking. From Tyler Road back to Wreck Curve Road. Hoping they could box Nikki and her attacker in. No one had known what they would find, or what they would do when they did.

The night and cold had been all around him.

None of them had had the answers—not until they could see Nikki for themselves.

He'd been terrified for Nikki. Phoenix had felt absolutely useless. Just like he had before—with his mother, with Perci, with his sisters when they were all being hurt before.

Phoenix didn't like how that had made him feel.

"I don't think anyone ever does. But that doesn't stop the relationships from building. Sometimes relationships have a way of happening when we are least ready for them. Sometimes good. Sometimes bad."

"Was your marriage good? Parker said he died."

"He did. I saw it happen. Motorcycle accident. I was in the car behind him when he was struck. Me and the girls. We were on our way to court to sign the final divorce papers, and my childcare canceled last minute. Not one of the best moments of

my life. One of the most devastating. I'll never forget seeing the
father of my children die right in front of my eyes. Ever. And
no. My marriage wasn't what could be considered *good*."

Phoenix flinched, imagining it. Her little girls were so
young...Younger even than Parker had been. "Yeah. I still see
my mom's face. Can't forget it. She haunts me."

"I can understand that, too. It's been two years for me, and I
still see every detail so clearly. I probably always will."

"I thought my dad hated me." The words just burst out.
Hell, even a bit of brownie had come spewing out of him. He
grabbed a napkin and wiped it up quickly.

But there was no judgment in her eyes.
Just...understanding.

It had been a while since someone had looked at him like
that. He was just Phoenix around here—the problem. Always
the problem. Never the solution.

"He was probably angry at the whole situation. Second-
guessing. And it sounds like he was horribly angry at himself
for a while. That's one of the...gifts...of hindsight, I think. And
one of the stages of grief is anger. We all are convinced there is
something we should have or could have done differently that
changed things. And we blame ourselves for it. If I had let
Lincoln reschedule our court date like he'd asked so he could go
on a date with a woman he'd been seeing since before I kicked
him out—he'd dragged it out four times before—he'd be alive
right now. I can't ever forget that. But...it was just bad circumstances that put him there. It's taken me a while to accept that."
She looked down at the little girl, patted her tiny back. "But
parents...we can be the angriest at ourselves, Phoenix. For what
we didn't do. Or even can't do. Sometimes that's enough to
keep you up at night."

"I kept thinking if I had just looked at the road better..."

"You've played it over and over in your dreams, and in your
dreams, of course, you fix things. Change things." She just kept

rocking, even when her daughter shifted, banged a small fist off Glenna's neck and kicked a bit. She just kept calmly rocking her daughter. It freaked him out a little, that calm. "But you can't. All you can do is take a deep breath and keep going."

It sounded so simple. But he'd been trying for five years. "I still miss her every day."

"I know. The memories, the hurt. I don't think they ever fully go away. I suspect your father feels the same way. He loved her very much."

"Yeah. He did." And that was at the heart of it. His dad had lost the woman he loved. "He lost her and it was *my* fault."

"No. It was the fault of an irresponsible woman who chose to knowingly do something so dangerous without regard to anyone else's safety—or her own. Just like what happened out there tonight wasn't your cousin's fault. The person who wanted to hurt her did so by his choice, not hers. She was just the unlucky woman who was in his way. Just like Lincoln's motorcycle was in the worst place at the worst possible time. The only one at fault that day was the driver who ignored the red light and spun out, striking Lincoln and three other cars. I was driving the fourth. The girls and I missed being hit by eight inches. I know in my heart Lincoln wouldn't have wanted that to happen to his daughters—or *me*—at all. Your mother...wouldn't want you to tear into yourself every day, letting anger consume you. No loving mother would. I wouldn't want that for my girls. I'd want them to go for life, for happiness, for love, with everything they had."

"I don't know if I can. I don't know if I even know how to be happy anymore." Phoenix looked at her, hoping that she had the answers. Shouldn't she have the answers? Didn't she deal with broken people all the time? "I'm not sure happiness even exists."

Glenna's daughter fussed, shifted. Glenna settled the kid back down. And just kept rocking. "It does. The first time I held my daughters, the first time they called me Mommy. When Robin, Rory—they are my best friends, by the way—when we are together laughing. When I know that someone I helped in my job is going to be ok. Making brownies with your brother, seeing the joy and discovery in his eyes. Holding your sisters' babies and having them smile at me. When your father's arms are around me. Happiness is all around us. We just have to let the walls down to see. You, Phoenix, have spent five years building those walls. You have two choices. Force them down or leave them up. And just like I told your aunt once—either way is going to hurt. You just have to decide which hurt you can deal with more. That's a choice we all have to make eventually. And it's a choice unique to each and every one of us."

Forty-Seven

PHIL CLIMBED OUT OF HIS BROTHER'S TRUCK AND waved Nick away. The cold bit into him. He didn't know if it was because of the falling adrenaline of the hours before, or because it was damned cold in Masterson tonight.

Nikki was safe. Already cuddled up to Hunter Louis Clark, of all the men in the world. Deliriously happy. Or she would be. Once she and Hunter stopped hurting so much. They'd be feeling the bruises of tonight for a long while to come.

Not just physically.

He was just damned glad they had found that girl in time. The idea that she had been running for her very life not even a mile from his house—and he hadn't known in time to do much good—showed him how precarious life truly was.

He slipped in through the kitchen door quietly. The light was still on. Someone, probably Pete, was still up. Waiting for him. His boy would have questions.

Pete was almost a man now. He'd wanted to be out there, but Phil had stopped him, told him to stay home—for his brothers, for the girls, and for Glenna. In case what Phil found had been devastating.

The boys would have needed Pete there. His son had under-stood that.

Phil would respect that, and answer those questions in return.

But it wasn't Pete. There was a beautiful woman still snuggling a sweet, sleeping little girl.

Right there, waiting for him.

Next to his oldest son.

"Glenna, honey, what are you still doing up?"

"Elly has a bit of an earache again tonight. We did hot cocoa, a small brownie, and snuggles. Phoenix and I have been talking."

"Nikki?" Phoenix asked, an odd look on his face that told Phil he had walked in at a bad time.

But there wasn't an answering look on Glenna's face. She didn't seem upset.

They hadn't been arguing, then. He...wasn't quite up to dealing with Phoenix *tonight*. He just wasn't.

"She's going to be fine. Mostly bruises. Hunter's been stitched back together. Heard Slater Davis has a touch of frost-bite. Guy was wearing boots, at least, but they weren't made for Wyoming. And he was out there quite a while. Walking through the snow."

"Slater Davis? The guy from the movies?" Glenna asked, quietly. "He was here?"

"Yes. Came back with Hunter. Damned glad he did. Nikki's best friend would have frozen to death out there tonight if he hadn't. Either her or Nikki. It would have been guaranteed for one or the other. Hunter couldn't have rescued them both. Slater carried Dusty a mile and a half up the road to Levi's." Phil reached out. Grabbed his son when the boy stood to start the coffee pot.

Phil yanked him closer. And just held him. They could have lost Nikki tonight.

Anything could happen to anyone at any time. Phil always tried to remember that. It took a moment, but Phoenix returned the embrace. "Dad? You ok?"

"I...hell, Phoenix, we could have lost Nikki out there tonight. Just because of some random quirk of fate. Just like we almost lost the girls so many times before. Or you the night Rutherford found you. I am not going to bed tonight without telling at least one of my kids that I love you. And if something happens to me and I'm not there in the morning—you make sure the rest of your brothers and sisters know it, too. I love you. Your mother loved you. And I will until the day I die. Nothing will ever change that. Not even for a moment."

Forty-Eight

PHOENIX JUST ABOUT LOST IT. THE EMOTION IN HIS dad's words...had tears threatening. Hell, he was twenty-two years old. He wasn't going to break down into an emotional mess and cry at his father's dining room table.

He pulled himself together, hugged his dad in return, and no matter how he wanted to cling to his dad like a kid no older than Parker, he stepped back.

He was a man now.

Time he acted like it. Stopped causing pain to the people who loved him. And they did love him. No matter what had happened that night, his dad loved him. As did his brothers and sisters.

Maybe his life wasn't in Masterson any longer, and to be honest, the thought of ever returning permanently was enough to have him breaking out in a cold sweat, but the people in this town, in his family, were his *life*. His world.

L.A. could never match that, even though he thought he was finding a part of himself there. But here, Masterson was *home*. *His dad* was home.

Phoenix hugged his dad again. Probably the first embrace he had instigated in five years.

It felt right.

Like it was supposed to.

When he pulled away, his gaze landed on Glenna. She'd just sat there, quietly rocking her kid, waiting.

There was a soft look in her eyes as she watched his father. One that said she understood more about his father than even his father did in that moment.

A look he'd seen in his sisters' eyes when they'd looked at the husbands they loved so much.

Love.

She'd said she had feelings for his dad.

Phoenix didn't doubt those feelings were real now.

"I should go upstairs," she said softly once Phoenix turned away to grab the coffee. It was decaf, but he suspected his dad needed warmed up after the night they'd had. "Put her in her bed."

"Don't go yet," Phoenix's father said. "I... Phoenix, you staying here tonight?"

Phoenix got the message. His dad wanted some alone time with the pretty lady. Needed it.

He had two choices here: make an ass out of himself or step aside and let his dad live his life on his own terms.

No matter what the changes that brought. Quit being a brat and let his dad do what he had to do to be *happy*. Even if that meant with the woman *not* Phoenix's mother.

Phoenix wanted his dad to be happy more than anything. His dad deserved it.

Phoenix looked at Glenna. "I can take her up if you want. I'm going to crash in Pete's spare bed for tonight. Rowland will probably want to check on Hunter in the morning. He's coming in on an early flight. Stick around for a few days. Handle...publicity. That kind of stuff. He's going to need me."

His dad nodded. Glenna stared at Phoenix for a moment. Like she was trying to decide if she could trust him with her daughter. Then she shifted forward. "She's in your old room. Across from the one I'm in. She has a favorite blanket she'll be looking for when she wakes."

Phoenix nodded. He took the little body and held her close, remembering how Parker used to be this small once. Parker was really the first baby Phoenix had ever cared for at all. He'd been eleven when Parker was born. The little girl was limp and sweaty in that weird way kids had.

He got an odd sort of comfort from that.

He left his dad behind, staring at the housekeeper like she was the answer to his dad's prayers, and carried the little girl to the room that had once been his own.

There was a pink, heart-shaped nightlight near the bed. He lowered the little girl—he still didn't remember which kid she was—to the toddler bed that had replaced the battered twin bed that he'd slept in for years. It was pink, too.

The pink was an odd contrast to the blue that the room had been for years. Pip had wanted to repaint it, but that hadn't happened. She'd moved in with Matt instead. And was happy.

All four of his sisters were happy now—in spite of what had happened before.

The same dresser he'd used from the time he was this kid's age was right there.

The fossil remains of old Power Rangers stickers stuck to the side were still visible in the dim light. Hell, that dresser was more than two decades old now. And it was still right there. Sturdy as it always had been.

Of course, it was—one of his uncles had made it himself years ago. For the baby that Phoenix had been.

He didn't know why that dresser stood out to him tonight. But it did.

It was just the damned dresser.

He covered the little girl up with her favorite blanket, that was right there on her bed, and tucked it over her shoulders. She was only like two or three or something, he thought. She was half the size of his niece Ivy who was five.

He was old enough to be this kid's father.

That sank in. Maybe he would have been a teenager at the time, but he could have a kid this age now. His mom had been nineteen when Phoebe had been born.

He could be this kid's father.

Could be totally responsible for a little life.

That sank in fast as the kid rolled on her belly and stuck her butt in the air, one small hand going to her mouth. She still sucked her thumb in her sleep. His mouth quirked at that.

She was just a baby.

Defenseless in a world she couldn't hope to understand.

With just Glenna to protect her.

Glenna and *his* dad now. Holding back the darkness of the world.

The darkness that had almost taken Nikki tonight.

Every kid deserved someone to protect them from that.

He tucked her stuffed animal in next to her, and dimmed the bedside lamp like he'd done in this room thousands of times before.

Phoenix pulled the door shut almost completely. There was a baby monitor on the dresser. It matched the monitor that had been sitting on his dad's kitchen table.

The dresser didn't look much like one fit for a little girl at all.

Phoenix headed to the room where his brother slept. Pete was sprawled over his twin bed in the corner, looking almost too big for it. There was another bed in there. Phoenix didn't know why the dork needed two beds instead of swapping it out for a double bed, but he was grateful it was in there.

With Glenna's girls everywhere now.

He hadn't wanted to bunk on the couch.

Maybe part of the problem was that he was a *man* now. And not a kid. But being here...brought it all right back to the surface, making him feel less like the man he'd like to think he was and more like the child he was afraid he'd never fully outgrow.

He'd walked away two years ago a child. Maybe a part of him became that child because he'd never accepted that it was time to put that behind him?

He didn't like the man he was anymore.

He had made things tough for his sisters and even tougher for his father. Phoenix wasn't proud of that.

Hell, Phoenix wasn't proud of the man he was becoming at all.

Maybe...maybe there was something he could do to change that.

Forty-Nine

THE INSTANT PHOENIX DISAPPEARED UP THE BACK steps to the rooms above, Phil acted. He didn't hesitate. He had his woman in his arms, holding her as tightly as he could.

Her arms tightened around his waist. "Are you ok?"

"I will be. Tonight just...too many memories. And it was too damned close out there." He just breathed her in. She smelled like Glenna...and brownies. He wished he could carry her upstairs and show her how much that made him want to taste that scent. But that wasn't going to happen yet.

Neither of them were comfortable being together while their kids slept in the next rooms. At least not until he got her to make a commitment to him. He wanted that more than anything. "I...want you to make this a permanent thing between us."

"What?" She pulled back to look at him with wide green eyes. Like he'd shocked her.

"I want you to consider marrying me when you are ready. I mean...tonight made me remember something I've known for a long time. Life is too short, too unpredictable to assume we'll have more tomorrows. I want you to know how I feel about you, and that I want this between us to be forever. And that means marriage. You, me, growing old together. My boys, your girls growing up together in this house. Me sharing my ever growing bevy of grandchildren with you for cuddles and kisses. You running around with Robin, and Rhea, and whoever else— keeping them all out of trouble."

"Phil?" Her hands tightened on his shirt. "You..."

"I want you...with me forever, Glenna. Right here." He placed one hand against the scar over his heart. "My heart beats for you now just as much as it beats for my kids and grandkids. I want you coming home to me at night. And I want to hold you close as we both grow old together. Right here."

And then he kissed her, leaned back...and waited.

Fifty

GLENNA STARED UP AT THE MAN LIKE HE HAD GONE completely crazy. Even if his words had echoed the thoughts she'd had while he was out there in the storm. "I..."

"I know I am rushing things, and I know this is probably not the way it should be asked, but I'm just...I can't lose you. And I want the right to tell the world exactly what you mean to me."

"We've only known each other six weeks," Glenna pointed out. "To the day."

"I know." He shot her a grin, looking like Patton in that moment. "But I have always been a bit impulsive. Definitely impatient."

"What if we are just caught up in things and something goes wrong?"

Her first marriage had been just as quick, just as impulsive as what he was offering her. And she had thought she loved Lincoln enough to ignore the problems between them. But this...it wasn't just her now.

Even if she did love the man far more than she had ever loved Lincoln. She was smarter now, more self-aware, certainly. She knew what she felt was real. But it wasn't just *her* now. And everything she did had to be for the girls. She would never do anything to destroy their happiness. "We have eleven kids between us to think about before we go making permanent decisions."

"What is there to think about? I love your girls as if they were mine already." His hand slipped up to cup her cheek. "And I know you love my boys, too. And they all love you. The girls —mine—have all told me how well you fit here. And how much they like you. Our families want us to be happy. I will take care of your girls like they are mine, no matter what. And I know you'll do the same for my boys, if anything happens to me before the youngest two are grown. And more than that, Glenna. I will love you until the day I die. You have my word on that. And I'm a Tyler. Our word is golden."

She found herself nodding. Agreeing to this crazy, crazy man. "I love you, Phil Tyler. But we are going to have to make sure *all* of the kids agree to this. Or we figure something else out. I'm not going to give you up either."

He gave a low laugh that shot heat straight through to her heart. His arms slipped around her waist, and he pulled her closer. Kissed her in a way that seared her straight to her toes. And then he was lifting her off her feet and setting her down on the kitchen table. And kissing her again.

When he pulled back to breathe, he asked one small question. "When?"

Six weeks. They'd known each other six weeks. But... "I want Robin and Rory and Robin's kids here. And my brother if he can get here. They are my family. And you'll need to talk to your kids. Make sure they are ok with this. So...two months from now. That would be...May. Or we can do June."

"Be a June bride?"

"Yes. I think that would work perfectly."

"Good. And in the meantime, there is a small cabin behind this place. It's technically my nephew Michael's. As soon as this snow melts, I'm going to take you up there. Spend the night, maybe even two. With no kids around. We'll get some of the girls to come spend the night with all the kids. We'll call it...an early honeymoon."

Glenna nodded. Then he was kissing her again. Right there in the middle of his kitchen table.

They didn't stop for breath until Elly's fussing came through the monitor. Glenna pulled back, as reality came crashing in again. "I'd better go check on her."

"We'll check on her, together."

Reality had come crashing back in—but now, she didn't have to face it alone.

Fifty-One

PHOENIX FOUND HIS FATHER WRAPPED UP AROUND the housekeeper, in the middle of the living room couch, early the next morning. Fortunately, this time, they had on most of their clothes. But his father's hands were under Glenna's sweater. They hadn't even changed out of their jeans. He stood in the door frame, just watching them for a moment.

They looked like they belonged together right there.

He turned, back to the kitchen, as the kids started trickling down the stairs. Parker was lecturing Glenna's oldest daughter about something.

"Nikki needed the Tylers. To rescue her," Parker said. Apparently, the kids had been discussing the night before. Phoenix winced, imagining what kind of drama Parker had invented to fill in the details.

His youngest brother was far more imaginative than any of the rest.

"I don't need no boy to come and rescue me," the oldest girl said hotly. Stubbornly. She looked like her mother in miniature. But she had a temper and an attitude at times. "Ever. I rescue myself."

"You are living in my house now, Evangeline. That means I'm like your big brother, and you are like a Tyler. Just like when we got Ivy. Being a brother means responsibility. Obligations." Well, Parker was right about that part. Phoenix couldn't argue that. "Tylers take care of Tylers. All the way from Uncle Bill down to me. It's just the way it is. That means that if you, Emmy, or Elly ever need rescued, me and Pat and Pete are supposed to do it. Phoenix, too, when he's here. Just like Ben and Gil and Fletcher went with Dad to rescue Nikki. Tylers take care of Tylers."

"We're not Tylers," the girl had to point out, again, as Patton and Pete came down behind her and Parker. Pete carried the youngest girl on his hip, and Patton kept the middle girl from running down the stairs and crashing like they all had so many times before. Phoenix still had a scar under his chin where he'd bounced off the bottom step years ago.

Then five kids and one almost man were staring at Phoenix. He waited for them to demand to know why he was there. Like he had no business being there.

"We can't find Dad or Glenna," Patton said, worry in his tone. "Did something else happen? Is that why you're here, instead?"

Hell, he was the one in charge for the moment, wasn't he? Well, being a brother had obligations, responsibilities. It was time he started living up to those.

"They are sleeping in the living room. They stayed up late talking after Dad got back." Phoenix gave them all his best in-charge stare, feeling like a total phony. "No one is to wake them up. She feeling better?" he asked of Pete as he settled the baby in the booster seat at the table. "She was really fussy last night."

"Elly's feeling a little warm again. Glenna might want to call Nate or Rhea. I think her ear infection is back." Pete fastened the kid in. Glenna's girls were daredevils. Phoenix had seen that one almost turn the chair over before. "So...I take it you and I are in charge of breakfast?"

That was it. Tylers doing what Tylers had to do. Getting things done. Taking care of each other.

Just like Phoenix had never left.

Phoenix laughed quietly as that gave him a sort of peace he never would have expected. "Yeah, I think we can manage it. Eggs and toast?"

"Sounds like a plan."

The older girl looked at Phoenix, a challenge on her face. "We're not Tylers, you know."

"Not yet," Phoenix told her. Evangeline—Evey. This one was Evey. The littlest one Pete had called Elly. That left...Emmy as the middle girl. He knew their names now. He wouldn't forget. "But you might be someday. Would that be so bad?"

She shrugged. "I don't know. Maybe not. I haven't decided yet."

There was a wariness in her eyes. A fear. Of change? Of the future? Maybe. That was something he could relate to. Their world had changed, too. Phoenix looked at the rest of the kids as they settled down at the table, waiting for breakfast. For the day to begin for all of them.

Looking as if they all belonged together.

Maybe they did. Maybe they had been put together because they were *meant* to be together.

After Phoebe arrived, ready to start the day, and Pete had woken their father and Glenna and sent those two upstairs to get ready for the day—before Pete and Patton had left to split their dad's chores up between them—Phoenix stepped back upstairs.

The door to his old room was still open. He slipped inside.

His eyes landed on those Power Rangers stickers. Before he even realized what he was doing, he was slipping the drawers free, and laying Elly's clothes neatly on her bed.

He carried the dresser and drawers downstairs and out to his dad's workshop. It could be heated by kerosene heaters, and he could open the doors for ventilation.

He was going to remove those stickers. Breathe new life into that old dresser.

It had a new purpose. Phoenix didn't need it now, but little Elly did.

After lighting the heaters, he went back inside and upstairs. Phoenix slipped into the room that had once been the twins.

Yes. There were two old dressers in there, too, just like he'd suspected. They had *Pip* and *Perci* stenciled in purple-and-pink letters that had faded with time. They had been stored in the basement for years, he thought. His dad had fished them out for these two.

They looked old and battered and faded.

It took him five minutes to empty both dressers.

They were small. Easy to carry. He was wrestling both down the stairs when his father found him.

"Care to explain what you are doing?" his dad asked quietly.

"Making a few changes around here." Phoenix kept going. He had his damned coat on, and it was hot in the kitchen. His dad grabbed his own coat and boots and slipped them on. Followed. "I'll need to find stencils somewhere. Of their names. But I think these will work better with some changes. Just because they are older than they look doesn't mean there isn't life left in them."

His dad snorted at that. They weren't talking about the dressers, and both men knew that. "No kidding."

Phoenix had the dressers in place. It would take some sanding to smooth them out, and he'd have to go to town to the hardware store, grab some paint. White for one, pink for another, and maybe that girlish light purple for the third. And letter stencils in contrasting colors. Just like Pip, Perci, Pan, and Phoebe once had. Little girls liked that kind of stuff.

"I see. Might check the school supplies for stencils. Phoebe is a bit of a hoarder for that stuff. Thought I saw some the other day."

"Do you think the littlest one will like white or pink best?" Something about that kid had stuck with him. Maybe because of all the kids, *she* was the only one young enough to be Phoenix's own.

Holding her had made him realize a few things last night.

He didn't need his father as much as that kid did right now. And those kids had found their way to his father for a reason. For all of them.

Instead of answering, his dad just pulled him close and hugged him again. "You are a good man, Phoenix Tyler. And I am proud to call you my son. Let me help you with this today, ok? There's something I need to talk to you about, anyway."

Phoenix shot his father a look, and he *knew*. Knew exactly what his father had on his mind. Just what he and Glenna had been talking about last night that ended up with his dad's hands copping a feel. "As long as I don't have to be the *maid of honor*, I'm good with it, Dad. Just...make sure you are happy, ok?"

That was exactly what he wanted, he realized. For them all to be happy again. To find peace. As he and his dad worked together, sanding down the dressers for three little girls, that was what he actually found. Peace.

It might only last for a little while. But he would find it again. And again.

Because that was exactly how life worked.

When they quit around lunch—and he texted Rowland back to tell him he was busy with his family and taking the day *off*— and they headed back inside, and he saw the look Glenna had in her eyes, that was when he understood.

He surprised both of them and himself by scooping her close for a hug. Wow. She felt smaller, more vulnerable than he would have thought. Not like the enemy at all. "Take care of him. Take care of them all."

"You'd better believe I'm going to do my best to do just that."

And she hugged him back. This woman who wasn't his mother but that his father loved.

Her girls would be Tylers. They would all be family, be taken care of. Be happy.

Because Tylers took care of Tylers, after all.

That was the way it was supposed to be. No matter who ended up being a Tyler. Or how they'd gotten there.

Tylers took care of Tylers. He wouldn't have it any other way.

Epilogue

HER FATHER HAD CALLED A FAMILY MEETING TWO mornings after Nikki had been found. Joel bundled her and Aria up into his sheriff SUV and drove them over the snow to the house where she had grown up. Her hand covered her stomach as the movement of the truck made her feel like she was riding a roller coaster today.

She smiled, remembering his face when she'd told him her news this morning.

Joel Masterson was going to be a father again. It was a bit earlier than they had planned or anticipated, but, well, some nights Joel was a bit too impatient for birth control. It had been bound to happen sooner or later. She was glad it was sooner, even as exhausted as she was.

Which...a new pregnancy explained exactly *why* she was so tired, too.

"You're smiling," her husband said as their daughter dozed in the back seat. "Good thoughts?"

"Yes. I want to tell them today. Today should start with good things." She had visited the doctor yesterday. Confirmed it. She had told Joel that morning after she had woken him and loved him.

They talked about possible names as they made the rest of the drive. The storm had ended. Everything was crisp and white and beautiful, everywhere she looked. Winnie, Parker's dog, greeted them on the porch. She was always the first one to greet them. Phoebe liked the continuity of it all. She patted the dog on the head, then did the same with Patton's dog, Wally, who was on the porch. Liberty mostly just stayed inside—that dog was the smart one, after all.

Dogs, chickens, goats, and a bunch of wild kids—that was what this place meant. *Home.* It was home, and it always would be.

Phoebe stepped inside, holding the door for her husband and daughter.

Her dad was there in the kitchen, like he almost always was, something taken apart in front of him on the table, waiting for him to fix it. It looked like...a remote control Jeep or something.

There was a pan of cinnamon rolls cooling on the counter. Tomato sauce simmered in the slow cooker, and something boiled on the stove.

Her sister Pan was at the sink, washing glaze off her hands. Talking to Glenna, who held baby Griffen close and loved where she stood next to the table. The sauce was probably one of those two women's doing—they spent a lot of time, Glenna and Pan, discussing recipes and things.

Nate was at the table, Perci holding little Elly while Nate looked in her ears with an otoscope.

Parker and his little posse greeted Phoebe and hugged her. Then turned toward their real purpose.

"Are they ready yet?" Parker demanded. Emmy and Evey and Ivy echoed the question. Parker's little shadows, those three.

Well...when he and Evey weren't arguing about who was actually in charge around here.

That was still open for debate with those two.

"Not yet," Pan said, shooing them from the kitchen. She looked at Phoebe. "Pip and Matt are in the living room with the rest of the babies. I figured they are responsible for making half the grandkids—they can handle babysitting duties. Keep them from making another too soon. I sent Levi in there, too. He needs that lesson, fast. At least until Griff is older. Much older."

Her dad just laughed. "I wouldn't mind at all."

"No, you probably won't." Phoebe did a small headcount. Someone was missing—three someones, actually. "Pete and Patton? And is that Phoenix's rental?"

"They are finishing up a project in the workshop," her dad said, an oddly proud look in his eyes. "For the girls."

Almost as if they'd heard him, the door opened. There the rest of her brothers were. Each one carried a small, freshly painted dresser.

They filed upstairs and returned five minutes later. To go right back outside and come back in with the matching drawers.

"Phoenix repainted the dressers for the girls. So they could have space of their own here," Glenna said softly. As Phoebe's father reached up and patted her on the back.

Let his hand linger.

"Lunch will be ready in five minutes," Pan said. "Think someone could set the table?"

Her dad moved his project. Pan wiped the table quickly. Phoebe opened the cabinet, started grabbing plates. She handed them to her brother-in-law Nate. Perci was in the rocking chair holding Elly now. Rocking her while Glenna stood nearby, rocking Griffen back to sleep in her own arms.

Phoebe loved this family so much.

There were more plates on the table than ever before. Her

dad was talking to Nate about what he'd have to do to add a leaf to the table. Before the babies got big enough to need their own chairs, instead of high chairs stuck in random places throughout the kitchen. Someone knocked on the door. Patton opened it as he was the last of her brothers to come down the stairs and was closest.

Phoebe's mother-in-law and her new husband stood there. Phoebe's father greeted them and invited them inside. "Just in time for lunch."

"Sure you have room for a few more? I was looking for Glenna. Looks like I found a whole bunch of somebodies to love," Rhea said. She leaned over and looked at Phoebe. "You feeling better today, sweetie?"

Phoebe nodded. "Loads."

She was thrilled Joel's mother was there today. It made things even better.

Within ten minutes the table was set, the food was being placed in the middle of it. And her father was calling all the kids to the kitchen. Pip and Matt and Levi came in, carrying Daniel and Davin and Marlowe and Poppy.

When they were all settled in and her dad had said a prayer, something he always did when they had a family dinner like this, Phoebe looked at him. She was just about ready to tell them she had an announcement, when her father stood.

The words died in her throat.

He looked at each one of them individually. Cleared his throat. And glanced at the woman next to him. He reached for Glenna. She reached for him. And her dad looked back down the large table at all of them. "Glenna and I have something to tell all of you."

Phoebe checked all of her siblings' faces quickly. Even Phoenix seemed ok right now. As their father told them how he felt for Glenna and how she felt for him, told them what the future held, Phoebe bit back her smile of pure happiness.

Her father was *happy* again. The way he deserved to be.

Her words a few minutes later made him even happier.

Just like she had known it would.

Her father wrapped his arms around Glenna right there at the table and kissed her quickly. Then turned to Phoebe and she found herself back in his strong arms again. Knowing everything was going to be ok.

Finally.

They were all going to be just fine.

What happened when Robin kissed Nick all those years ago?

THE FIRST THING NICK Tyler saw when he entered the building of the trucking company he ran with his nephew was a small, but perfect feminine rear end encased in khaki trousers. It was stuck straight up in the air, while the woman attached to it bent under the old metal desk one of his nieces had sourced for them to use in the main office.

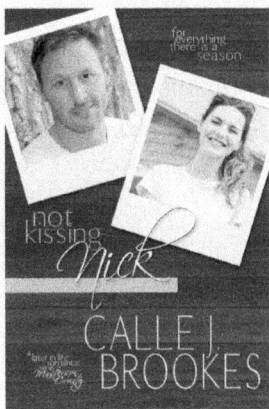

The woman was muttering something dire as she reached for whatever she just couldn't grab.

"I could help you with that, if you'd like," Nick said. He mostly just wanted to figure out who it was under his desk. It was a very nice rear end, after all.

The woman yelped, bumped her head, and stood quickly. She stared at him.

He stared back.

She had hair that warred between red and brown that she'd pulled up in a twist. Big light blue eyes stared at him and a soft pink mouth parted slightly. An absolutely perfect looking mouth.

She was damned gorgeous. It was rather hard to miss.

"Nick? Wow. I think we both got old." She gave a rueful grin that told him *exactly* who she was. She had sweet dimples and a smile that was crooked enough to say she liked to break the rules just a little bit.

Just like before.

Robin. It really was her. Staring right back at him.

He had always liked how little Robin Patton looked.

She hadn't changed much. Just gotten older. A little curvier, but that was a good thing. A very good thing from where he was standing.

She had to be thirty-eight or nine now.

"Robin, it's good to see you."

"You, too, Nick." She eyed him warily. Like she was afraid of him? Robin hadn't been afraid of anything. She knew what she wanted and she went after it.

She'd been pure hell on wheels once.

Until that damned Sheriff Gunderson had started harassing her. She'd been just a kid. Gunderson had been old enough to be her father. Nick had never forgotten the terror in her eyes that night he and Phil had found her and Gunderson alongside the highway.

That had been the deciding factor. She'd left town then—and hadn't come back.

The last place he'd expected to see her was in his own office, acting as if she belonged there.

His nephew Chandler had let him know he'd hired a new secretary last week. Nick had been so busy with booking a large run that he hadn't paid much attention.

Nick suspected he was looking at his new secretary right

now.

Damn.

"Settling in ok?" He wasn't sure he wanted *Robin Patton* working with him every single day. She was going to be highly distracting.

Just like before.

She remembered. Just like he did.

Robin had been taunting him ...tempting him on purpose.

He could see the memories of those two stolen kisses in the blue eyes staring at him now. She'd been so sweet—and it had been *Robin* who had kissed him. Had put those hands of hers places she had no business putting them—back then.

Nick had done the right thing both times. Probably a bit more harshly than he should have. He'd just...wanted her to understand. She had to stay away from him back then. Or he would do something totally stupid. She hadn't been ready. He'd known that. He was nine years older—when she'd been almost nineteen, that had mattered.

This woman had been enough to tempt a saint into doing something totally stupid. Nick had never missed *that.*

The heat in her cheeks intensified.

"It is good to see you. I mean that," Nick said, softly.

Seeing her, yes. He wouldn't mind seeing a lot more of her. She was buttoned up to the neck in a prissy little purple blouse that hid far more than it revealed. Far cry from what she'd been wearing the last time she'd practically accosted him.

He'd always remembered her in that little blue tank top and the cut off shorts that had revealed far, far too much of Robin.

This schoolmarm getup was the exact opposite of that.

Did she realize how that tempted a man, too? His fingers itched to hit those tiny buttons and just yank them off forever. See what that silky smooth skin looked like beneath. To touch that skin...

Having her in his office, thirty feet away from his own desk?

That was going to prove problematic. Unless… "So what have you been up to over the last twenty years? Married, sixteen kids?"

Please let her say she had a six-foot-seven former linebacker husband just waiting for her to get home. Someone who'd kick Nick's ass for the thoughts he was having right now. Someone who'd bring her lunch every day just so he could glower at Nick and Chandler and make certain they were behaving around the temptress that was Robin Patton.

That might be enough to have Nick behaving. Maybe.

She gave a soft smile. She looked so…shy. Robin had never been shy with him before. "I was married, but he passed away. I have three kids, though. Nine-year-old twin boys, and a little girl. She's two-and-a-half—but going on thirty-five. She looks just like my sister."

He had never imagined her having kids. In his head, she was still the almost girl she'd been back then. The one who had tempted and tormented him and had him breaking out in a sweat.

He'd always wondered what happened to the girl she had been. "What are their names?"

"Philip and Wesley, and Rebecca. We call her Becky."

He saw the pain there and he reacted to the familiar names —her sister, her brother-in-law, and Wesley had been her grandfather's name. The grandfather she and her sister had adored. Before he could stop himself, he cupped her cheek in one hand.

Her skin was just as smooth as it had been twenty years ago.

Traces of the girl remained, but…Robin was all grown up now. Beautiful. Gorgeous. Right in front of him. Widowed.

Every male cell of him was standing on alert, shouting *Robin! It's Robin! Grab hold now!*

Like they'd been waiting for her all along.

"I'm sorry about your sister, honey." Losing her sister Becky in a car accident five years ago had been devastating for all of them. Nick had feared his brother would never recover.

"Yeah, me, too."

He was half-afraid she'd start crying. That had sheer panic going through him. "But you are home for good now?"

She nodded, a tentative smile on her lips. "I think so. Thank you for the job. I really needed it."

"Thank you. We needed someone we can trust in here. I'm trying to get things up and running so I can kick Chandler to the curb." Then...it would just be him and Robin in the office every day. Together.

Working side by side. Almost touching.

Well, his office was down the hall, but...it was close enough.

He was never going to survive this.

Startled blue eyes met his now. "Why would you do that?"

"It's no secret around the family. He wants a restaurant of his own, but was already committed to taking over here before I convinced him to let me buy in. I'm going to take over here and shove him off the ledge. The whole family is scheming to get him moving on his restaurant. He's a bit risk adverse, that nephew of mine."

"Aren't we all?" She stepped back firmly.

Nick really didn't want to let her get too far away.

The exact opposite.

It had been a long time, *years,* since he'd felt instant attraction to a beautiful—*available*—woman.

It figured that it would be her.

She smelled nice. She looked nice. And the idea that she was going to be right there in his office—and there wasn't a big burly husband to keep him in check...

Robin Patton always had tempted the hell out of him. From the time she'd been almost nineteen to the day she'd run from town and Clive Gunderson, with four hundred dollar bills his brother had given her in her pocket.

Nick's four hundred dollars. He'd given it to his brother for her.

He hadn't known any other way to help her, except by taking her with him when he'd left Masterson for the army when his leave was up.

He'd seriously considered it that night. Just...taking her with him and leaving Masterson forever. Marrying her, signing up for base housing. Building a life with a not-quite-nineteen-year-old girl who had never seen more than little Masterson County.

She wouldn't have been ready for the life of a military wife, on her own so much, away from their families, friends. *Home*.

Far from it.

And he wouldn't have wanted her with him just to escape a man who had no business stalking her.

She'd just been too damned young back then.

But...he wasn't too old for her now.

There was no husband in the picture for her. No wife in the picture for him. No Clive Gunderson terrifying her.

Robin wasn't too young now.

Nick wasn't going to survive.

What had Phil been thinking, talking Chandler into hiring *her*?

He had only one real answer.

His brother had done it on purpose.

Phil was out to get him. Out to put pure temptation right in front of Nick, just to mess with Nick's head.

Because Phil could—and was evil that way.

Phil was getting back at Nick now for something. That was the only rational explanation.

Probably for Nick's continual flirting with Phil's new 'housekeeper' whenever he saw her.

Nick couldn't help himself—one, it annoyed his widowed older brother, and two, Glenna was an extremely attractive woman.

Phil had noticed that himself.

That's why Glenna now wore an engagement ring on her left hand—and had a beautiful glow whenever she looked at Nick's older brother.

Yes. Phil had to be after revenge.

Well played, big brother. Well played, indeed…

Also by Calle J. Brookes

ROMANTIC SUSPENSE

PAVAD: FBI ROMANTIC SUSPENSE

Beginning (Prequel 1)

Waiting (Prequel 2)

Watching

Wanting

Second Chances

Hunting

Running

Redeeming

Revealing

Stalking

Ghosting

Burning

Gathering

Falling

Hiding

Seeking

FINLEY CREEK SERIES

TRILOGY ONE (TEXAS STATE POLICE)

Her Best Friend's Keeper

Hearing her Cries (releasing 2022)

LATER IN LIFE CONTEMPORARY

THERE IS A SEASON...

Just Loving *Gerald*

Forever Holding *Phil (May 2022)*

Not Kissing *Nick (June 2022)*

Never Chasing *Charlie (Summer 2022)*

SUSPENSE/THRILLER

PAVAD: FBI CASE FILES

PAVAD: FBI Case Files #0001

"Knocked Out"

PAVAD: FBI Case Files #0002

"Knocked Down"

PAVAD: FBI Case Files #0003

"Knocked Around"

PAVAD: FBI Case Files #0004

"White Out"

PAVAD: FBI Case Files #0005

"Buried Secrets"

Calle has several free reads available at

www.**CalleJBrookesReads.com**

For my grandfather, the best man I have ever known.

You will be missed.

Oct. 2015

For my grandmother, who gave me the courage to try. Without you and your love of romance, I never would have made it this far.

Feb. 2016

For my papaw, whose children loved him deeply, and will always miss him.

Oct. 2017

Calle J. Brookes enjoys crafting paranormal romance and romantic suspense. She reads almost every genre except horror. She spends most of her time juggling family life and writing while reminding herself that she can't spend all of her time in the worlds found within books. CJ loves to be contacted by her readers via email and at **www.CalleJBrookes.com**. When not at home writing stories of adventure and wrangling with two border collies and a beagle puppy, CJ is off in her RV somewhere exploring the beautiful world we live in, along with her husband of she can't remember how many years and their child.

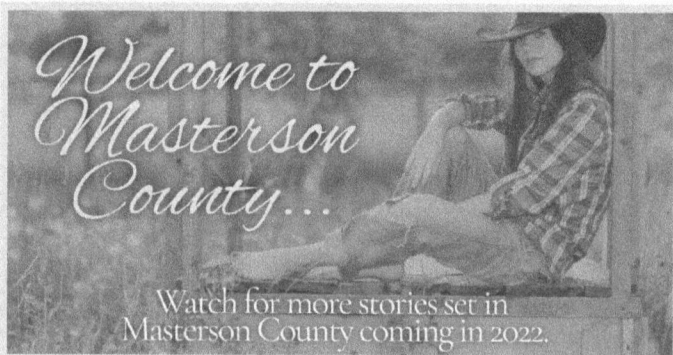

Welcome to Masterson County...

Watch for more stories set in Masterson County coming in 2022.

Calle has several scenes that were removed from her books available at her blog: www.callejbrookesreads.com.

Calle updates the blog on a regular basis with free reads, excerpts from upcoming books, deleted and bonus scenes, and on-going serial stories.

The next serial will begin in 2022, as soon as Calle decides whether it's a PAVAD story, Masterson, or Finley Creek.

Follow the **blog** for the most up-to-date news about Calle's books and bonus freebies, or sign up for Calle's **newsletter** to be notified about new releases when they go live. (Calle only emails a newsletter with new release information).

To follow the blog visit:

To sign up for the newsletter visit:

Lightning Source UK Ltd.
Milton Keynes UK
UKHW010741060223
416537UK00003B/976